Cover Design and Interior Format

SUBMITTING FOR Christmas

EM BROWN

Dedicated to nasty women…

CHAPTER ONE

—◆◇◆◇◆—

MILDRED ABBOTT WINCED AS HER mother emitted a wail of despair. She had no wish to cause her mother pain, but in this, her relief exceeded her guilt.

"You must speak to Haversham again," Mrs. Abbott insisted.

But Mr. Abbott had settled into his favorite armchair before the hearth, and having done so, was unlikely to rise for some time.

"He has decided to depart for Scotland tomorrow."

"All the more reason to speak to him before it is too late," his wife said, her voice high and shrill with desperation.

Mr. Abbott shook his head. "It would do no good. It is not Haversham who must change his mind. It is Alastair."

Mildred drew in a deep breath. Her cousin had done it. Though he had initially refused to intervene in the matter of her engagement, in the end he had brought about the result she had hoped for. She had erred in accepting Mr. Haversham's proposal, and only the Marquess of Alastair had the position and the influence to alter the arrangement without too much consequence falling upon the formerly engaged couple.

"Surely something can be done," Mrs. Abbott persisted. "Haversham was partial to our Millie. I know it."

"Apparently not enough to acquiesce to the marriage settlements required by Alastair."

Mrs. Abbott wrung her hands. "I know not why the Marquess has decided to concern himself in this matter when he has never concerned himself with us before. Why now?"

"I suppose it is my fault for having approached him with a request for Millie's dowry."

"Nevertheless, he is not the one who need marry Haversham!"

Millie suppressed a smile at the idea of her cousin marrying Haversham. The two men could not be more unalike. The latter was an obsequious dandy who had modest connections, the former was an arrogant and, many deemed, cold-hearted man of quality.

Mr. Abbott reached for his newspaper. "Well, as he is the one providing Millie's dowry, he has a right to interfere."

Mrs. Abbott gave another wail. "Now who will have Millie? It is not as if she has a queue of men wishing to court her!"

Mildred took no offense at this, for it was true. Though there was much she could yet do to improve her appearance, she knew her beauty to be middling. She had neither soft tresses, long lashes nor the slender figure desired by most. She had other qualities that would serve a husband well, but there was a part of her that few would find acceptable.

Beneath her facade of sense and goodness, churned a dark and prurient nature. She had been much ashamed of this part of her until Alastair's aunt, Lady Katherine, had come across her in a compromising way. In agony that she might have ruined her family, Mildred had been greatly astonished when Lady Katherine had comforted her and, later, *encouraged* her.

It had been an immense relief to Mildred to find that she was not alone in her wicked proclivities, and that these were shared by a woman whom she respected and admired.

"Now Millie will never marry!" Mrs. Abbott lamented as she sank to the sofa.

Mildred took a seat beside her mother and passed her a handkerchief to dab her eyes. Spinsterhood was not a prospect that daunted Mildred, save for the grief that her parents might experience. She was their only child, and as they had but the most modest of means despite their connection to Andre d'Aubigne, Marquess of Alastair, their only hope of seeing their daughter provided for was through marriage. For this reason, Mildred had accepted Haversham's hand.

But regret had set in within minutes of her acceptance. That night, she had decided that she would rather face spinsterhood than marry Haversham. If a husband could not be had—she wondered that she could ever find the right man to marry—she would find employment as a governess or lady's companion. She could appeal for assistance to Lady Katherine, who had taken a liking to her. She would secure her own future.

"I feel quite ill," Mrs. Abbott said.

"Shall I assist you to bed, Mama?" Mildred asked.

"No, no. I am too aggrieved to move."

"Millie's dowry is still in place," Mr. Abbott assured his wife without glancing from his paper. "Alastair has even raised the amount to four thousand pounds. I expect we will see more suitors than we care to entertain."

Mrs. Abbott leaped to her feet. "Four thousand pounds! Truly? Why did you not speak of this first? Why, with such a grand sum, Millie can have much better than Haversham."

Mildred sat, stunned. She had not requested this of Alastair, and she doubted that her father, who had been more than pleased with half the amount, would have dared request more than had been initially granted.

Mrs. Abbott practically danced about the drawing room. "I must tell Mrs. Porter of this! She will not believe it! At last, my brother's marriage to a d'Aubigne has produced some benefit for us. I can almost forgive him now for his lack of consideration. He ought to have provided for the rest of us instead of keeping the riches of the d'Aubigne family to himself."

Mildred said nothing, for Richard, Mrs. Abbott's older brother, had passed away many years ago and was thus beyond receiving her clemency. And Mildred believed that her uncle, perhaps ashamed of his humble background, acted to protect the d'Aubignes from clamoring relatives.

"Richard would have us believe that Alastair had not a generous bone in his body, but at four thousand pounds... Well, I suppose it makes up for his lack of attention to us all these years. It amazes me how little he has done for us. Millie is his cousin, after all."

"By marriage, not blood," Mildred reminded her mother.

"Oh! The difference ought not matter. I had hoped the two of you could have formed a bond as you are not so very different in age."

Mildred flushed. Her mother could never know that, for one night, a special bond *of the most intimate nature* had been had between Mildred and Alastair, but not the sort Mrs. Abbott would have ever conceived.

Mildred pressed her legs tighter together as she recalled how delightfully the Marquess had attended to the flesh between her thighs *with his tongue*. And she, in turn, had taken his member into her mouth. How exquisitely naughty it had all been. How amazingly rapturous.

Mildred had tried not to recall too often her night at Château Follet, nee the Château Debauchery, when she had submitted her body to Alastair. But resistance was futile. It had been the most memorable event of her life. She had replayed every moment, and each recollection produced a heat inside of her. In the quiet of her bedchambers, she had fondled herself to the memories. She had found her own touch wanting compared to his, but she dared not dream for an encore. She still marveled that she had managed to harry him into taking her and fulfilling her deepest, darkest desires.

She had resolved, despite Alastair's belief to the contrary, that how they regarded and interacted with each other would be unchanged.

"You think our relationship can remain the same after what happened?" Alastair had challenged her the morning after their congress.

"Why not?"

"Your naivety is charming at best."

"Well, we are not often in each other's company," she had replied. "The night will hold little significance for you after you have had a tumble with Miss Hollingsworth or whom-ever you choose next. I daresay you will have forgotten the night altogether after your next visit here."

She wondered if he had forgotten, then told herself that of course he had. She was but one of many whom he, a known rake, had taken to bed, and had done so, undoubtedly, with reluctance.

"I wonder if we should invite Mr. Carleton to dinner?" Mrs. Abbott mused aloud. "I think he could be persuaded to take an interest in Millie, now that her dowry is the sum of four thousand pounds."

"Mr. Carleton!" Mildred shuddered. The man was worse than Haversham.

"His family's merchant business does very well, I under-stand."

"He lobbied *against* the abolition of the slave trade."

"He was not the only one, my girl. And do not suppose that you can disparage such prospects simply because you have a dowry of four thousand. Four thousand!" she cried, her voice shrill this time from glee. "Mrs. Porter had thought her nephew too good for the likes of Millie, but she will have to reconsider now that Millie has *four thousand pounds!*"

Mildred frowned. Mrs. Porter's nephew, a portly fellow afflicted by gout and who disdained of bluestockings and the need for women to display their intelligence, was hardly a better prospect than Carleton. This would not do. This would not do at all. She saw a dinner table full of prospective suitors her mother had invited, hours upon hours of making polite conversation with dull-wits and no end to her mother's efforts at matchmaking.

"But I think Mr. Winslow, her neighbor, may also take an interest in Millie. He had been courting Miss Bennett, but I heard she had taken a fancy to some dandy."

"I thought Winslow to be courting Miss Stephenson," Mr. Abbott commented.

"That was *last* year, shortly after he was courting Miss Drury. Or was it Miss Laney he had been partial to?"

Mildred leaped to her feet. "I think I shall go for a walk."

"Alone?" Mr. Abbott inquired, looking up from his paper, perhaps fearing he would be compelled to keep her company, though it was her custom to take solitary walks.

"I may stop to visit Mrs. Bridges," Mildred replied, regretting the necessity to fib. In truth, she intended to pay a visit to her cousin.

"Do not make it a long visit, as dusk will be upon you before you realize."

"Yes, Papa."

As she exited the drawing room, she heard her mother say, "Perhaps I shall take tea with Mrs. Elliott tomorrow. She has a sea captain staying with her. He is quite a bit older than Mildred, and his complexion reminds me of worn leather, but that is to be expected when one spends as many days beneath the sun as he must…"

Mildred threw on a pelisse, quickly pinned on her bonnet, and slipped on her gloves as she hustled out the door. It was no short distance to Grosvenor Square, where Alastair lived, but she was unafraid of walking.

She could not permit Alastair to increase her dowry to such an amount. It was beyond generous, a trait she—or anyone else—would not have expected to exist in the Marquess. What could have possibly prompted such a gesture from him? She doubted her father, who had been quite nervous at requesting a dowry in the first place and would likely not have done it if not for the prodding of his wife, would have ventured to ask for it.

But why would Alastair have volunteered to raise her dowry? Lest his aunt had persuaded him to? Mildred supposed this must be so. Lady Katherine had a kind heart and was partial to Mildred. She would have to thank her ladyship, but they simply could not accept so generous a dowry. Mildred shuddered to think whom else Mrs. Abbott had in store for her.

Mildred quickened her steps. Though she would rather not make any further requests of her cousin, especially when she had exacted quite a bit from him already, she simply had to convince Alastair to rescind the four thousand pounds.

CHAPTER TWO

—⬥⬥⬥—

MILDRED SCANNED THE GAMING HALL looking for her cousin. She spotted him at the faro table flanked on either side by two beauties. The flaxen-haired beauty to his right leaned often toward him, her shoulder grazing his every other minute. The woman to his left had wide rouged lips, and the longest lashes Mildred had ever seen. She batted them at Alastair from behind her ivory-handled fan.

The attentions of the two women did not surprise Mildred, for the Marquess of Alastair had a striking, if not imposing, countenance framed by the d'Aubigne curls of ebony and all the qualities desired in form for his sex: a broad chest, square shoulders, and posture that accentuated his height. Though Mildred had not been struck at first by his handsomeness, for his eyes did not glimmer with charm and he did not often smile, since their encounter at Château Follet, she had come to find him compelling in other ways.

"Please let Lord Alastair know that his cousin wishes to speak to him," Mildred informed the footman. She could tell the Marquess was engrossed in his game, for he paid the two women beside him little attention. Mildred would not be surprised if he should choose to ignore her request for an audience. His butler, in informing her of his lordship's whereabouts, had warned her that he would not wish to be disturbed. For that reason, Mildred had kept her bonnet and coat.

She drew in a sharp breath as she watched the footman deliver her message to Alastair. Her cousin glanced up from his cards, he seemed neither pleased nor displeased, and Mildred decided it mattered not if he should see her. If he declined, she could always write him a letter expressing her gratitude. Indeed, she wondered at the necessity in coming to deliver her thanks in person. She wondered at her own eagerness. Had it been simply an excuse to see him?

The footman returned, and Mildred braced herself to receive the news that the Marquess was indisposed, but the servant said, "If it pleases you, miss, you may await his lordship in the parlor down the hall."

She released the breath she had been holding and answered, "Yes, of course."

She followed the footman to the parlor. After he had left her alone, she sauntered about the small but nicely appointed room. She had not the patience to sit upon the sofa in the middle of the room. Why, of a sudden, did she feel nervous? It was silly. She was merely going to thank him.

She had only felt such nerves one other time with her cousin. It was the night she had approached him at his aunt Katherine's birthday to request his assistance in getting out of her engagement with Haversham. She did not often find him as intimidating as others would.

But there was no denying that the nature of their relationship had changed since that fateful night at the Château Debauchery. Not only had she lifted her skirts to him, she had done so in the most wicked and wanton fashion.

To keep her mind from straying into the past, she studied the baroque longcase clock in the corner, wandered to the hearth to warm her gloved hands at the fire, and viewed herself in the looking glass above the mantel. She was glad she was comely enough such that Alastair had capitulated to her desires. She had fancied that perhaps he had even desired her a little, enough to be aroused, though she had heard that his sex required little in the way of arousal and could be titillated by the prospect of congress with any woman, even if she was not the most striking.

"What is amiss?"

She whirled about to face her cousin. Now that he was in closer proximity, he appeared more imposing. She tried not to recall how strong and heavy his body had felt against her.

"Nothing," she answered, gratified that his voice had carried more concern than was his custom.

"Then why are you here, Millie?"

Now he sounded displeased.

"I came first to thank you," she said, refusing to be intimidated by his mood. "Father said that Haversham departs for Scotland on the morrow."

"Good riddance. May I suggest that you pick your next husband more carefully?"

"Of course. I rather think that I shall not be accepting any more proposals for some time."

He made no reply, and she suspected that he desired to return to the card tables, but she could not leave without addressing her other request.

"I would have written a letter to express my heartfelt thanks, but I was uncertain when it would reach you, and I did not think that it would have adequately communicated the sincerity of my gratitude."

"No thanks are necessary."

Knowing the best manner of thanks she could provide at the moment was allowing him to return to his cards, and perhaps the two beauties that awaited him, Mildred could not resist staying him for just a minute. "But you will have it, nonetheless, for it is the proper and polite response to express gratitude where it is due."

"And when have you known me to care for what is proper and polite?"

She grinned. "*I* will do what is right and bestow my thanks. *You* may choose to receive it however you wish."

"Consider yourself acquitted of any further obligation. What is your second reason for coming, and I daresay I hope there is not a third?"

"Worry not. I do not plan to keep you long, and you may return to your vices soon. I have but a simple request."

He raised his brows. "Another request?"

She flushed, realizing she had imposed upon him rather often of late. "It shall be my last."

"I pray it so or it might become a habit."

Ignoring his rudeness, she forged on. "I should dearly appreciate it if you were to return my dowry to the original amount of two thousand pounds—or even less."

He stared at her.

"I know not what my father might have said," she continued, "but two thousand pounds was more than kind."

He crossed his arms. "Never before have I encountered anyone whom it is so difficult to bestow money to. You spoke of what is proper and polite. It would be proper and polite of you to accept my donation and be grateful for it."

"I am grateful for your generosity but would not encroach upon it further."

"Alas, it is not for you to do so. Your father has accepted the new dowry on behalf of your family."

"Well, of course he did!"

"Because anyone of middling intelligence would."

She drew in a sharp breath, then saw a glimmer in his eyes that allowed her to release her breath. "Alastair, you have been more than kind, but four thousand pounds is beyond the pale. I do not merit such a sum."

"There are plenty of unworthy women with far larger

dowries than you."

She suppressed a scowl. "But why the need to increase the amount?"

"Because you merit better than Haversham."

"But four thousand pounds will attract every Tom, Dick and Harry."

"That is not my problem, Millie."

"But you—" She forced herself to take a breath. How the man tried her civility!

"You are a clever girl. I expect you will learn the art of rejecting your suitors without badly wounding their hearts—or pride."

"I've no wish to. Dealing with Haversham was enough for me."

"Millie, you have made several requests of me, and I have no desire to encourage further requests from you. Thus, my answer is *no*."

Her mouth hung agape before she landed upon another strategy. "If that is your position, then you shall have to suffer my gratitude and many, many expressions of it—and often—profusely—for such a level of generosity deserves praise and—"

To her surprise, he drew up before her, and the air surrounding them suddenly constricted.

"Are you threatening me?" he growled.

Her heart palpitated rapidly. His proximity left her without words.

"If we were at Château Follet right now…" he began.

She quivered at the unnamed possibilities. Though she had told herself that one too many glasses of wine had contributed to the amorous affect her cousin had upon her, the truth was rather different, as evidenced by the melting sensation she currently felt.

Seeing that he had silenced her, he retreated a pace. "Are

we done, Millie?"

Never had gathering words proved so difficult, but she managed a "yes."

Pulling her shawl tighter about her, she made for the doors.

"Wait."

The command sent her hurling back to that night at Château Follett, when she had followed his directives in delicious delight. Her heart still beating rapidly, she dared not look at him, not wanting him to see the effect he had upon her.

"How did you arrive?" he inquired.

She turned around only after she had enough composure in hand. "I walked here by foot."

He looked toward the window. The skies outside had begun to darken. "The hour is late. You should take my carriage."

"Thank you for the offer, but I am not daunted by the distance home."

"Did you come alone?"

"Yes, but—"

"Then you will take my carriage."

"I enjoy walking."

The cool air would help dampen the warmth swirling inside her.

He gave her a penetrating stare, and for a moment, she thought he might finish the thought he'd had earlier and specify a punishment for her refusal. She shivered at such a prospect. Would he take the crop to her? The flogger?

"I will not require my carriage for some time," he said, removing any last obstacle to her acceptance. "Time enough for my driver to take you home and return."

"Very well," she declared. Then, wanting to reclaim a little of her pride, she dared to irk him. "I accept your hospitality. Let it not be said that the Marquess of Alastair lacks kindness."

His countenance darkened, and he grumbled, "Consider yourself fortunate, Millie, that we are *not* at Château Follett."

His words took her breath once more. She wanted a ready retort but could not conjure one. She watched him open the doors and call to a footman to have his carriage ready.

"Good night, Millie," Alastair said before heading back to the card room.

She was glad he did not tarry to keep her company while she waited for his carriage. His presence rattled her more than she liked. Now that he had mentioned Château Follett, there was no holding back from venturing there in her mind.

CHAPTER THREE

---◈◈◈---

A LASTAIR FAVORED THE BLOND, THOUGH it mat-
tered little which of the two lightskirts he selected to fuck
in the grounds behind the gaming hall. Miss Woodwin—or
perhaps it was Woodwiss; he could not remember nor cared to
remember—gasped as he pinned her against the building with
his body.

"Your lordship," she breathed, "you are presumptuous."

Despite the dim lighting from a half-clouded moon, he
could see the sparkle of desire in her eyes. She had been
brushing her body against his all evening; brushing his fore-
arm as she reached for a card; tapping his shoulder to inform
him of his turn, though he had known bloody well each
time it was his turn; and bumping into his leg beneath the
table whenever she shifted in her seat.

"Am I?" he returned, cupping her chin and lifting her gaze
to meet his. "Would you rather I take my leave?"

Her lips parted but returned no words. He already knew
the answer, and had asked his question to curtail any protests
she felt obligated to feign. Her bosom heaved beneath him,
and when the silence continued, he lowered his mouth to
take her lips. He could taste and smell the three glasses of
port she had consumed. A gentleman would have hesitated
to press his advantage with an inebriated woman. But she
had known precisely what she did, having begun her flir-

tations before the first glass, the port providing her a ready pretext for her later actions.

And Alastair was no gentleman.

Were it not for his status in polite society and his endowments in form and countenance, no woman of reason would wish to tempt him. And, in general, he found their sex rather wanting in judgment. He had thought his cousin, Millie, whose uncle had married his aunt, to be an exception. But she had surprised him by accepting the proposal of a rather stupid fellow, from which she then suffered buyer's remorse and sought *his* intervention to dissolve the engagement.

Millie surprised him in more ways than one. He remembered how astonished he had been, sitting at one end of the dining table at Château Follet, to see her at the other end. She must have seen him enter the dining room, for she had been in some haste to depart the table, running into a maid carrying a tureen of gravy. He had followed her out and found her, soaked in gravy, hiding behind a sofa in the drawing room.

He had intended to sacrifice his own plans to partake of the carnal merriment at the Château Follet to see her safely away from the den of debauchery, but she had stubbornly refused. He could not believe that his aunt, though she had been the one to introduce him to Château Follet, would have facilitated Mildred's participation. It had been the most confounding night, one in which the proprietress, Madame Follet, in finding him and Millie at odds, dared accuse him of sanctimony. Never before had he been so vexed by their sex. He had implored them to be reasonable:

"*Marguerite, pray be reasonable. You do Miss Abbott no favors by permitting her to stay.*"

"*Andre, she is my guest, not yours. Your aunt—*"

"*Katherine is far too enamored with this place and in want of discretion.*"

Marguerite arched her slender brows. "Andre, this is most unlike you. And because we are good friends, I will dare to say that I find your position rather selfish."

She astounded him. She deemed him selfish when he was willing to sacrifice his long-awaited weekend at the château to protect his cousin?

His look of vexation did not daunt Marguerite. She continued, "Oui. You have partaken readily of the pleasures here but would deny the opportunity to another?"

He tried a different approach. "I ask you, as a friend, I beg of you to see the soundness of my actions."

"Your aunt is my friend as well, and I am loath to disappoint her."

They had all lost reason, he decided. All three women. Women he had hitherto thought sensible—especially Millie.

"I do not mean to disparage you or the château, Marguerite," he said, unrelenting, "but it is not worth the risk for Miss Abbott."

"Sir, you presume too much on my behalf," Millie said.

Marguerite put a gentle hand upon his arm. "It is trés amusing to see you fret in the manner of an old woman, but I assure you that all will be well."

His vexation trapped all words. If she were not the hostess, he would have a few choice words for her.

Marguerite turned to escort Millie from the room, but he stopped them. Addressing Millie, he said, "Do not be a fool. I am willing to chaperone you home, but I may not be so generously inclined later."

She straightened. "I thank you for your kind offer, Alastair, but it is not necessary."

His nostrils flared. The chit should be grateful for his selfless gesture!

"Stop such idiocy, Millie. You do not fully comprehend what transpires here."

"I have been well informed by both your aunt and Madame Follet."

"And the wiser course would be for you to reconsider!"

"How is it the wiser course for me but not for you?" she cried.

"Are you truly asking such a daft question? I had thought you more sensible than that."

She flushed with indignation. "I intended to draw attention to your hypocrisy with my question."

"It is not my hypocrisy but that of society's. The consequences fall much more harshly upon the female sex."

"But here at Château Follet, the sexes are equal," declared Marguerite. "It is a quality you appreciate, mon chéri, and benefit from."

"But how will Millie benefit?"

"In the same manner you do, but of course."

"That is different."

"How?"

Why were these women asking such ridiculous question? Did they truly require him to state the obvious?

"Certain ruin awaits her if she is discovered."

"That has yet to happen with a guest."

"She won't like it here."

Millie breathed in sharply. "Surely that is for me to determine."

"I assure you this is no place for you. My dear aunt has not been here in some time and forgets the nature of the acts here would appall you."

"I am not easily frightened or appalled."

"Millie, don't be a dolt."

"I object to your condescension, sir!"

"It is for your own good. You know no one here. What man do you expect will pair with you?"

He saw her eyes widen and regretted the harshness of his words, but it was warranted if he was to talk sense into her.

She looked ready to attack him or cry. "You think no one will desire me?"

"That is not what I said."

"It is what you meant!"

He fumed because her accusation was not entirely untrue. "The men here—their expectations are different."

Her bottom lip quivered. "If I am not selected, then I will take pleasure in watching others."

Her response stunned him into silence.

"Andre, I protest," Marguerite intervened. "Miss Abbott has a right to be here as much as you do, and I dare say, if you do not leave her be, I shall have to ask you to leave."

If not for his promise to grant Katherine's birthday wish, in which she, fearing for his loneliness, had requested that he take the concerns of someone in hand, he would have left Millie to her own devices, would have let her suffer the consequences of her foolishness.

Or would he? The memory of the Viscount Devon still made his blood boil. He could not have, in good conscience, allowed Millie to be his prey. Any inaction on his part was tantamount to feeding a defenseless hare to a hawk. Millie had thought the man charming, but Alastair would sooner trust a thief.

And so he had granted Katherine's request and would see to Millie's safety, but she had thwarted his intentions to lock her in her chambers for the night, away from the clutches of Lord Devon.

Alastair had thought he could convince Millie to be reasonable. The pleasures of Château Follet were not worth the risk to her honor. But she had surprised him yet again by revealing that she was no longer in possession of her virtue. He had been flabbergasted at the time, but, upon reflection, he found the revelation rather intriguing. Few people surprised him.

"Something amuses you, your lordship?" Miss Woodwiss asked.

He started.

"I think that the first smile you have displayed all evening," she commented, visibly pleased with the prospect of being the source of his pleasure.

Recalling himself, he gave a half growl and closed her mouth with his. The less she talked, the better. He ground his erection against her. Thinking back on Château Follet had doubled his ardor. A shiver went down his legs as he recalled one of their most memorable exchanges after he had taken her.

"But I had hoped to take your member," she said.

"Millie, did you think we were engaged in something other than congress?"

"Into my mouth."

His eyes steeled, and he pressed his lips into a firm line. "I will not degrade you further."

"But there is titillation in degradation, is there not? Is it not supremely wanton and wicked to take that man's part and place it where nature had not intended?"

"Millie, the hour is late."

"Do you not enjoy the act?"

"Millie, I will not allow you to browbeat me into this."

"Browbeat? No. I merely wish to entice you. I have received some instruction in this and am no novice."

He shook his head. "Good God, Millie. When I discover this wretch who has turned you…"

"Turned me 'what?' Into you?"

He was ready to spank her, though he had already punished her backside.

"I will ask no more of you after this," she promised.

"You are asking to—to take me into your mouth…"

She gave him a broad smile. "Yes. Please. My lord."

He uttered an oath beneath his breath. Before he could answer, she had sunk to her knees before him. She eyed his crotch hungrily.

"You might even be pleasantly surprised," she said. "I may be as good as or better than Miss Hollingsworth might have been."

She reached a hand to the buttons of his fall, but he caught her wrist.

"Millie—"

She pouted. "Come. It is not as if we are engaging in sin."

"Not engaging in sin?" he exclaimed, incredulous.

"Further sin. We have done the worst of it already."

With her other hand, she cupped his groin, making him groan. "I am not one given to generous doses of conscience, and you would lay to waste my attempts at goodness."

"I never invited you to be what you are not."

He appreciated this in Millie. Outside the Château Follet, women were constantly trying to change him. His sisters wanted him to end his profligacy. Even Katherine wished he could be more caring of others. And those who set their caps at him…he knew what they were about. They hoped to tempt him into marriage and harbored romantic notions that he would forsake his rakish ways in favor of love. Millie was far too sensible for such silly fancies.

He wondered if Miss Woodwin would swallow cock as readily as Millie had. Not knowing the blond well, he would not inquire. Instead, he lifted her skirts and cupped a bare thigh. She sighed against his mouth. The sensation of Millie's mouth about his cock had been nothing short of marvelous. She was not practiced in the art of taking cockmeat, but she had approached it with much vigor.

He moved his hand between Miss Woodwin's thighs and found the moisture of her desire. Her breath became short and shallow as he fondled her. In his mind, he saw Millie moving up and down his shaft, gagging at times when his cock struck the back of her throat, but relentlessly soldiering on. He did not doubt that, with more practice, Millie could be quite adept at eating cockmeat.

His groin ready to burst, Alastair could wait no longer. He unbuttoned his fall and, lifting Miss Woodwiss, buried himself inside her. She gave a grunt of satisfaction. He thrust his hips, pinning her to the wall.

He had come close to spending in Millie's mouth but could not bring himself to do so. He had opted to carry her to the bed and return the pleasure he had received. Her quim had tasted fine, her body deliciously responding to every lick and suckle. After she had spent, he had sheathed himself a second time inside her.

His cods boiled, wanting release, but he held off until he sensed Miss Woodwiss approaching her pinnacle.

"Ya, ya, ya," she mumbled as she rode his cock.

He bucked his hips faster, tightening his hold on her, for Miss Woodwiss was as light as a ragdoll. He remembered how Millie, a quick student, had known to ask his permission before spending. He remembered how she had met his thrusts, how their bodies had formed an easy rhythm.

Miss Woodwiss cried out as her body fell into paroxysms. When she had done shuddering, he pulled himself out of her and set her down. Aiming his cock away from her, he jerked at his member till his seed shot into the ground. They recovered in silence, she leaning against the wall to catch her breath, and he wiping himself with his handkerchief.

"Will you be here tomorrow evening?" Miss Woodwin asked.

"I think not," he responded as he replaced his fall. It had not been his intention to satisfy his lust with anyone tonight, but the appearance of Millie had changed all that. The memory of her and Château Follet had stayed with him longer than he cared to entertain.

For this reason, he had doubled her dowry. The sooner she found a husband, the better. Of course he would have liked to see her well settled, but it was also best that he be done with his cousin once and for all.

CHAPTER FOUR

SEEING THAT HER MOTHER WALKED her way with Mr. Carleton beside her, Mildred slipped into the corridor of the Grenville home and went to hide in the music room.

"Your pardon, I did not realize the room was being used," she said to the debonair young man, who seemed equally surprised by the woman who had rushed into the room and swiftly closed the doors behind her. Not wanting to return and risk being found by her mother, she looked about the room, which contained a pianoforte, a harpsichord, two violins, and harp. "Are you musically inclined?"

He looked sheepish. "In truth, I don't play at all. I was seeking refuge—I mean to say, solitude. Do you play?"

"A little, but I must confess that I did not make my way in here in search of an instrument."

He lifted his brows and appeared a little relieved.

"I am not one given to much socializing," she explained further.

"Nor am I."

"You are a friend of the Grenvilles?"

"I am a friend of Mr. Harris, and staying with him, and he is a close friend of Mr. Grenville. I am George Winston."

She returned a curtsy to his bow. "Mildred Abbott. My family and the Grenvilles have known each other for a long time, and I all but grew up with their daughter Jane."

They regarded each other for a few seconds in silence before he asked, "Would you care to play?"

She made her way to the pianoforte and sat down. "You may regret your invitation, for my skills are limited."

He went to stand near. "I cannot cast stones, for I do not play at all. Anyone who has taken the time to learn a musical instrument deserves praise."

"That is very kind of you to say," she said as she selected Mozart's 'Fantasy and Sonata in C minor', "but I am quite tolerant of criticism. I know I did not practice as much as my instructor would have liked."

After she had completed the piece, with only a few minor errors, he clapped his hands, saying, "That was marvelous. You were being modest when you said you played only a little."

"I selected a rather easy composition."

"Are you quite difficult to compliment?"

She might have received this question as impertinent, but he spoke in such an easy, gentle manner, that she almost felt guilty for not accepting his praise.

"Your pardon. I did not mean to be rude."

"No offense taken, Miss Abbott. If I played as well as you, I should be deliriously happy with myself. Granted I am no expert at the pianoforte."

"I suppose I do appreciate that my family was able to afford a music instructor for me."

"I imagine you possessed other talents that you deem your-self 'a little' skilled at."

"Lest you think I am all modesty, I will boast that my French is quite good, but I am a horrible dancer. My dance instructor was even more cross with me than my music instructor."

He chuckled. "I would hazard that you are more modesty than not. I expect that if I were to witness you on the dance floor, you would not be nearly as bad as you think."

"Oh, I assure you I am."

He chuckled again, and his eyes seemed to sparkle when he smiled. "I suppose we shall have the chance to ascertain if you are accurate in your assessment or if I am correct that you underestimate yourself."

She shook her head. "I don't often dance."

It was a true statement. She did not often get asked to dance, though that had changed in recent months, thanks to Alastair. She tried not to think of her cousin every time Mr. Carleton or Mr. Porter approached her, but she would not have been in this position if not for Alastair.

"Do you not care for it?"

"I like the activity fine. I would participate more often if I were more skilled at it."

"I suppose I am more selfish in that I consider myself middling in my dancing skills, but my enjoyment of the activity exceeds what guilt I may have from inflicting my inferior abilities upon an unsuspecting partner."

It was Millie's turn to chuckle. "Imagine if we should both take to the dance floor. What havoc we might cause!"

He perked and beamed at her. "What a delightful notion! We should attempt just such a thing!"

She shook her head. "I could not."

"Ah, because you are a better person than I and would not impose upon others that which you believe would be a poor performance."

In truth, Mildred had hoped to remain closeted in the music room till all the dancing had past, but that was rather wishful thinking. She could not disappear for such a length of time without raising brows and appearing rude.

"You think too well of me," she replied to him. "It is because I would rather observe the elegance of those more graceful than I."

"I gather there is little chance, then, that you would accept my request to dance?"

She studied him, wondering if he was sincere in his desire to dance with her. She found herself rather tempted, for he had such an affable manner and the most charming smile.

"Indeed," she answered. "You seem a nice fellow, and I would not subject you to my poor dancing skills."

"If you underestimate your dancing skills as much as you do your skills at the pianoforte, then I should think you a rather good dancer."

"I would not take the chance, were I you. There are enough others here tonight who would assuredly be better than I."

"Even if you are a poor dancer, I would rather have you for a partner because it is quite clear to me that you are a woman of intelligence and wit. And I would sooner have a partner with whom I can converse well than a woman with whom I can dance well."

She shared the same sentiments, and would not mind being in Mr. Winston's company. Certainly, she would prefer dancing with him than the likes of Carleton or Porter. "Very well, but you have been warned."

"Splendid!"

"I shall make your middling abilities appear worse than they are."

"That does not concern me in the least." He glanced toward the door. "I suppose I ought to rejoin the others. I would not wish my host to think I had deserted him."

She drew in a fortifying breath. She was not ready to brave the Carletons and Porters but supposed she had to follow suit with Winston. When he presented his hand to assist her to her feet, she accepted it. He held on to her hand longer than she would have expected.

"I suppose it would not do for us to be seen walking from this room together," he said.

"Most assuredly."

He released her hand, and she felt a little wistful at its loss. "Ladies first, then. I shall follow and find you for a reel—or would you prefer the quadrille?"

"The quadrille, please."

"The quadrille it is."

Mildred took her leave with steps light and happy. The evening no longer presented to be as dreary as she had thought.

CHAPTER FIVE

---◆◆◆◆---

"WHAT DO YOU KNOW OF Mr. Winston," Jane asked of Mildred as they stood against the wall waiting for the dancing to begin. "The gentleman staying with Mr. Harris. He seemed a handsome fellow."

Mildred scanned the room but did not see him.

"I should say he is the most handsome of bachelors here," added Mary.

"I prefer Mr. Wiggins, but Mr. Winston would certainly be second in my opinion. But I should not be surprised if he takes an interest in Mildred more than anyone."

"In me?" Mildred felt an inner glow as she recalled how her hand had rested in his.

"Yes! All the bachelors seem to have taken an interest in you, now that you have a dowry of four thousand pounds."

Mary heaved an envious sigh. "How lucky you are, Millie, to have such a generous cousin in the Marquess of Alastair."

"She is lucky to have such a cousin, dowry or not."

Perplexed, Mary raised her brows.

"You have not met the Marquess, but you would understand what I mean if you had." Jane gave a mischievous smile.

"He is very handsome then?"

"Oh, he is more than that."

"He has not the best of reputations," said Mildred, feeling a little traitorous in speaking poorly of her cousin, but she spoke to convince herself as much as Mary.

"He cannot be all bad if he granted you such a generous dowry."

"He should despair to hear you speak so well of him," Mildred smiled. She frowned as she saw Mr. Carleton approach. "But I had rather he not be quite so generous."

"Why would you not? I think you must have more suitors now than even Miss Rose."

Yes, and she is none too happy about that," said Mary with a giggle.

"Miss Abbott," treated Mr. Carleton, a gentleman upon whom grey was not the best of hues. He wore a touch too much pomade in his hair, but was otherwise decent in appearance. "May I have the honor of the first dance?"

Before she could answer, Mr. Porter had arrived and said, "I had thought to ask the same, but I will settle for a reel."

"What say you, Miss Abbott? I think the quartet will begin to play any moment."

Mildred hesitated, wanting to say that she felt too fatigued for dancing, but she was looking forward to taking the floor with Mr. Winston. She supposed she could tolerate one dance each with Mr. Carlton and Mr. Porter.

"Remember you promised the gig to me," a voice behind her said.

Mildred turned her head and perked to see Mr. Winston.

Jane poked her subtly in the ribs as if to say, "I knew it."

"That is correct," Mildred said. "I did reserve the quadrille for Mr. Winston."

"Then I will have the next dance," said Mr. Carleton.

"Or, if I may be presumptuous—" Mr. Porter interjected.

Mildred imagined if Alastair could see the nettled state she was in, he would only be amused that he had produced such a fuss. He would have not an ounce of sympathy.

From across the room, she could see her mother talking to

Mrs. Harrington as she pointed first toward Mr. Carleton, then at Mr. Porter. Then into her line of sight came Miss Hannah Rose, dressed in a gown that might have featured in the most recent issue of *The Lady's Magazine.*

"There you are. We wondered where you had gone off to," she addressed Mr. Winston, then noticing Mildred, her smile fell, but she recovered in the presence of others. "Why, Mildred, that gown looks quite charming upon you. I think it my favorite among all your gowns. I can see why you chose to wear it last week at the Westbrook soirée, and the week before that at Mrs. Wilmington's dinner. If I had that gown, I would be tempted to wear it often as well, but then people may think it my *only* gown."

Mildred only smiled, for she was accustomed to these sorts of compliments from Hannah. Miss Rose was not a pretty young woman, though she had large eyes and long lashes. Three of her teeth were crooked, but she did not often smile with open lips. Her complexion was middling, and her lips protruded forward, but she carried herself as if she were a beauty, and that convinced many others that she was just that.

"I wonder that you do not acquire many more gowns, now that you have a dowry of four thousand pounds?" Jane asked.

Mildred looked sharply at her friend. She knew Jane spoke to irritate Hannah, but she would rather Jane did not trumpet the facts of her dowry.

Beside her, Mr. Winston raised a brow.

Jane ignored or did not notice the look from her friend. "How fortunate you are, Millie, that you have the *Marquess* of Alastair for a cousin. Why, you nearly have the connections of Miss Rose here, whom I understand has a great uncle who is an *earl.*"

Mildred suppressed a groan. As Hannah often flaunted her family's connections, Jane knew full well whom the Rose family was related to.

Hannah's eyes narrowed before conceding, "It does not compare to being related to a d'Aubigne."

"By marriage only," Mildred said. "My uncle was Lady Katherine's second husband. The d'Aubigne blood does not run in my veins."

"Even if the present Marquess of Alastair has a repute that would make any *decent* person blush and hesitate to boast his name," she finished with a hard stare and a tight-lipped smile directed at Jane.

Jane frowned and visibly struggled for a retort, given they were in company.

"Shall we take to the dance floor?" Mildred asked Mr. Winston.

"Yes," he replied eagerly, perhaps as relieved as she to be departing

Miss Rose appeared startled, but she did not want for a partner and was soon besieged by men asking her to dance. As others followed onto the dance floor, Mildred took her position facing Mr. Winston.

"I beg your pardon," he said.

She gave him a puzzled look.

"It appears you do not look forward to this dance, and I fear I had cajoled you into this earlier."

"No, no, I am fine. I was merely thinking of…less pleasant thoughts. My mind was not on dancing."

He returned a sympathetic smile. "I rather wish I were back in the music room, too."

His statement made her chuckle.

"I should consider myself fortunate to have ensnared the first dance," he went on to say as the music began.

"You are," she said in jest, "for, as I've said, I prefer to watch."

"I was referring to your many suitors."

"Oh. You mistake the men. They are not my suitors."

They took their turn in the first figure.

"No? Then it is commonplace for men to quarrel over a dance with you?"

"They are more interested in my dowry than in dancing with me."

"For a young lady with an impressive dowry, you behave with surprising modesty."

"All ladies of sizable dowries must be overbearing?"

"I suppose I have that prejudice. As you are a d'Aubigne, I admit to having fully expected pretension and condescension."

They awaited the other couple before resuming their discourse.

"I am not a d'Aubigne. My uncle married the aunt of the present Marquess of Alastair."

"That would make the Marquess your cousin."

"By marriage. We are not blood relatives, and our situations in society are quite different. You know the d'Aubigne family?"

"I was at Oxford with Andre d'Aubigne. He was two years my senior, and I do not think he took any notice of me, but I admired him from afar. He was quite the batsman at cricket. Do you see much of the Marquess?"

"No. There are not many occasions for us to meet."

It was a true statement for the most part. Their time at the Château Follet had been an anomaly.

"There are few occasions and little company that merit his tolerance, but, forgive me, I should not speak ill of your cousin. He was that way at Oxford, and he must be a different man now that he is a marquess."

"It would seem not." She nearly added that Alastair tolerated gaming hells better than he tolerated his family.

They moved on to other subjects after that. Mr. Winston

danced with sufficient grace despite his prior assertions to the contrary, and when he held her hand, she found his hold warm and comfortable. She was rather sorry to see the dance come to an end.

"I was right," Mr. Winston declared as he led her off the floor. "You are a much better dancer than you give yourself credit for."

"And you as well."

"Not only did we not make fools of ourselves, I think we presented a decent pair."

She smiled and would have accepted a second dance with him if he had asked, but he had not the chance. She was not surprised. A handsome and charming man, his attention was quickly engaged by many others, including Miss Rose. But Millie fancied he glanced her way every now and then. The pleasantness of their exchange lasted the remainder of the evening, and even accepting dances with Mr. Carleton and Mr. Porter was not as insufferable as she would have thought.

CHAPTER SIX

WHEN ALASTAIR CAME INTO HIS townhouse and received word from his butler that a "lady awaited," he thought it might be Millie. Few women would dare seek him out at his home. But he had not heard from Millie in some time and presumed she had abandoned hopes of persuading him to change her dowry. After their meeting in the gaming hall, she had written him twice with reasoning, threats, cajoling, and pleas.

He had responded by advising her to desist or he should be tempted to double her dowry to *eight* thousand pounds.

He had not heard from her since.

But the woman sitting in his drawing room was not Millie, alas. It was his eldest sister, Louisa, who bore no small resemblance to him. She had the ebony d'Aubigne tresses, sharp eyes, and strong bone structure. She stood taller than the average member of the fair sex, and with her ridiculously large ostrich plume in her bonnet, it appeared she stretched from floor to ceiling.

"Andre," she greeted at his entrance, then wrinkled her nose. "You smell of horse."

Having just arrived, he had not yet changed out of his riding clothes and boots.

"Have you lost all your manners?" she asked with a critical lift of the brow. "I may be your sister, but I am still a lady, and you know perfectly well a gentleman would not receive a lady smelling of horse."

Not bothering to point out that *she* had chosen to call on *him*, and without warning, he returned, "Would you rather I take the time to don a different wardrobe?"

He had no qualms in keeping his sister waiting.

She relented. "I haven't all day. I waited nearly half an hour as it is."

"Then praise the stars, for I nearly chose to ride out to Camden. Your wait then would have lasted hours."

"Your butler assured me you would be home before then, for you are expecting Mr. Kittredge."

"Kittredge does not mind waiting for me as long as he has access to my cellar." He went to pour himself a brandy from the sideboard and nearly considered offering Louisa a glass, though he knew full well she detested the drinks of his sex. She watched him in silence, no doubt waiting for him to inquire into her health or, at the least, the purpose for her visit.

"Do you plan to spend Michaelmas with our aunt?" she blurted when it was plain he had no intention of making an inquiry of any kind.

"No." He set his glass down at his writing table and picked up the letters of the day to review.

"It is not because you have yourself some opera singer here in town for a mistress? Surely you can command better than an opera singer."

Louisa did not approve of his having a mistress at all, but she had voiced this too often to deaf ears and was thus left with criticizing his choice in whom he tumbled.

"Did you come all this way to talk to me of an opera singer?" he asked, opening one of the letters.

She bristled. "Of course not! I asked if you intended to spend Michaelmas in the country with Katherine."

"And I gave you my answer."

"It affords me some refuge but, still, I think I cannot decline. I have not your ability to disregard what is proper. Were she not our only aunt, I should have arrived at some ready excuse to respond with my regrets. I would sooner accept an invitation from our uncle Herbert. Caroline said she can tolerate but a few hours with Katherine, let alone an entire sennight."

Caroline was his other sister, whom Alastair had even less regard for. Louisa could be critical and condescending, but Caroline added vanity to these qualities. She would spare no expense for her carriage, baubles, and lace, but would berate her housekeeper for spending a penny too much on butter.

"I do not think Katherine would care if you accepted her invitation or not," he said, hoping to end their dialogue.

Louisa huffed. "What a thing to say! Is that what she relayed to you?"

"Katherine is far too wise and well-mannered to confide such a thing to me, for she knows all too well that I lack the manners to pretend niceties where none exist."

His sister pursed her lips, not knowing what to make of his statement but wanting to know where Katherine stood in regards to her niece. "Your words imply that Katherine invited us out of obligation and not from a desire to have our company."

"I intended to imply that you should have no reservations in refusing her invitation," he replied without looking up from his letter.

She sniffed, "Well, when I heard that she had also invited the Abbotts, I knew for certain that I had no wish to go."

He paused. Millie had been invited to spend Michaelmas at Edenmoor?

"I shall never understand why she pays such heed to her poor relations."

"They are our relations as well."

Louisa gave a despairing groan. "They are all of such little consequence."

"Richard was a good man."

"I will grant you he was uncommonly decent for a man of his background, but marrying him does not require her to consort with all of his siblings, especially the Abbotts. I wonder that Katherine tolerates them."

"She is partial to the daughter," he said slowly.

"As are you, I take it, for I understand you are providing her a dowry of *four thousand pounds.*"

Here was the real reason Louisa had come to see him, he thought to himself.

"Four thousand pounds!" she reiterated when he said nothing. "That is more than that family has seen in their lifetime, I'll wager."

"Probably so."

She huffed again at his indifference. "What possessed you to grant such a sum to Miss Abbott? You realize that all of Richard's poor relations will be making requests of you now."

"They had been doing so long before I underwrote a dowry for Miss Abbott."

"And have you always been this generous?"

"Not at all."

"Then I fail to see the sense in such an extraordinary gift. Why, it is equal to the dowry for my Emily, and that is not as it should be."

"Very little in life is as it should be."

"Then you mean to go through with it?"

"Why would I not?" He immediately regretted his response, for though he meant the question to be rhetorical, he had invited an answer from Louisa.

"Because it is preposterous! Miss Abbott is not the sort

of young lady that ought to have a dowry of four thousand pounds."

"It would be bad form for me to withdraw it now."

"Since when do you care about good form?" she cried.

"Withdrawing now would be devastating to the family, and even I am not so cruel."

"But everyone or anyone would understand that it was a grave error on your part. They would not fault you for attempting to correct it."

"Then I have far too much pride to admit I could make so large an error." He was beginning to be more than a little irritated with Louisa. He knew he could provide no answer, short of delivering what she wanted, that would satisfy her.

"Then reduce it to a more sensible amount. I understand you had initially set it at two thousand pounds. Two thousand pounds is perfectly sufficient. Why you saw the necessity to increase it is bewildering."

"You may chalk it up to old age, the onset of madness, or inebriation, I have no intention of retracting."

She twisted her hands in frustration. "Then I suppose, if you are in such a generous mood of late, that I should request an amount for my Emily. A dowry of six or eight thousand pounds would be fair."

"As you pointed out, a dowry of two thousand pounds is 'perfectly sufficient.'"

She bristled. "Sufficient for Miss Abbott. But now that she is at four thousand pounds, it appears all wrong if my Emily, a d'Aubigne, does not have a dowry commensurate with her station."

"If you wish your daughter to have a dowry of six or eight thousand pounds, then talk to your husband and not to me. Your situation allows you to afford that amount."

" Two thousand pounds is no insignificant amount to us, but it is for you. And why should the Abbotts be the recipients of your generosity and not your own sister."

He set his letters down and finished off his brandy. If Louisa stayed much longer, he would require a second glass. "Because you are not in need of the money."

"But you have not granted anyone else in need such a magnanimous gift."

Louisa spoke true, and he had at one time reasoned to himself that he had granted Mr. Abbott's request to avoid having to deal with the man further, but that would not be the whole truth. He met his sister's stare and smiled. "It amused me."

"Amused you?"

"Yes, and I can assure that whatever answer I provide to your questions will not satisfy you, and only serve to exasperate you further. As such, I suggest you curtail this conversation so that you are not completely overwhelmed with vexation."

Affronted, she huffed with her mouth agog. He was a little surprised she was not, by now, accustomed to his impertinence.

"That is all the response I am to receive?" she asked.

"Yes."

She had exhausted his patience, and he was in no mood to entertain her further. He had a preponderance of correspondence to respond to before he left town with Kittredge to go hunting in the country.

"As your sister, I merit better!"

"No doubt you do, Louisa, but as you have often pointed out, I am both ungenerous and impolite."

"And well you deserve those labels!"

He did not bat an eye. Both his sisters had married well and needed naught from him. Louisa's daughters would have no trouble finding husbands of good standing.

"You will regret your actions," she said, "when you are

besieged by requests from your relatives and anyone who thinks they may claim a connection to you."

"Madam, I am besieged more by my own sisters than by distant connections."

At that, she threw up her hands and turned on her heels. Before she crossed the threshold, she turned around and waved a finger at him. "If you persist in such heartless disregard for your own family, then I shall wash my hands of you. I will, Andre! And when you are old and alone, you will come to reconsider your youthful recklessness and be sorry that you permitted all this to come to pass!"

Whirling about, she stormed from the room.

When she was gone, Alastair took a relieved breath. Louisa was fortunate he did not voice his true thoughts on her vanity and lack of interest in her relations. The latter, however, he owned he shared with his sister. He could not be certain why he had tolerated Millie. Perhaps because she neither tried to tempt him nor judge him, lest he had provoked her, in which case he had warranted her criticism. He remembered how cross she had been with him at Château Follet. He had been quite overbearing. Yet how easily they had fallen into their roles of domination and submission.

Her soft and supple body had withstood his attentions well. Her lips had yielded deliciously beneath his. Her cunnie had welcomed his cock with a marvelous heat. The area of his crotch tightened as he recalled how her cunnie had clenched his member as she spent.

In the glow of rapture, she had looked beautiful, though he had not found her striking before. In the morning hours following their night of wicked indulgence, he had had ample time to observe her while she slept and began to appreciate the suppleness of her body. He remembered his concern that she might wake with regrets or have developed an infatuation with him. He had been impressed with her lack of sentimentality. It was not what he expected from her sex.

"You have no regrets?" he asked.

"I am fully content with what has transpired," Millie replied.

"You will think differently with time."

"You are presumptuous, sir."

"There are few who would dare speak to me in such a manner, and fewer who could do so without raising my ire."

If they had not resumed their identities as Alastair and Millie, he would have taught her more courtesy. A spanking or a flogging would do nicely.

She lowered her gaze for a few seconds. "Your pardon, but, really, Alastair, you do not know me well enough to make such a claim. In truth, I am quite surprised that you seem to harbor more shame than I."

The thought seemed to amuse her, and he bristled. "I was only worried for your sake. My sex can dispense with guilt much more easily than yours, especially over matters of the flesh."

She was silent in thought. "Am I more the wanton jade if I harbor no repentance or shame? Am I a...slut?"

He groaned, and he felt another unsettling tug at his crotch. He had thought such sensations would not have persisted past the night.

"Millie, that is not at all what I intended with my words! I applaud that you honored the natural cravings inside you and sought to fulfill them without fear."

"You tried to stop me."

"That was before I knew you had already forsaken your virtue!"

"Then you have no need to worry of me, though I appreciate your concern. It is quite hopeful that you may not be as unredeemable as society deems you to be."

He growled at her teasing smile. Women. If he had had a choice, he would have selected one of his own sex to fulfill Katherine's birthday wish.

"My dear cousin," Millie said. "I will forever be grateful to you for last night. My one fear is that you will henceforth be awkward *in my presence.*"

"*You think our relationship can remain the same after what happened?*"

"*Why not?*"

"*Your naivety is charming at best.*"

As he recalled their exchanges at Château Follet, he considered that perhaps he should accept his aunt's invitation to spend Michaelmas at Edenmoor, but he reminded himself that doing so would require him to suffer the company of his sisters and their husbands. Hunting with Kittredge would be much more preferable.

CHAPTER SEVEN

───◈◈◈───

A LASTAIR STIFFENED AS HE AND Kittredge entered the main room of the Dante Club, for he saw, sitting in a tall wingchair beside the hearth, the Viscount Devon. The man had charmed Mildred at the Château Follet, and Alastair shuddered to think what would have happened had he not been present to rescue her from the Viscount's clutches.

"That fellow must be a new member," Kittredge said, following Alastair's gaze. "You don't appear too pleased to see him."

"I am not," Alastair affirmed.

"Who is he?"

"The Viscount Devon, a cad."

"That would be the pot calling the kettle black," Kittredge laughed.

Mildred had said something similar when he had attempted to raise her doubts of the man.

As if sensing he was the object of their attention, Devon looked toward Alastair. A flicker of recognition passed through his countenance before he returned to his friend.

"Shall we start with brag?" Kittredge inquired. "We can take the table farthest from this Devon fellow. Mr. Thistlewood has acquired some port that he believes to be the best the club has ever purchased."

When they had sat at a card table and saw no signs of the

manager, Kittredge rose to find the man. Alastair sat with his back to the fireplace but heard the Viscount approach the table.

"We meet again," Devon said. "Alastair, is it not?"

Alastair returned a silent stare.

"May I?" Devon did not wait for a response before pulling out one of the chairs at the table. He sat down and spotted the cards. "What is your pleasure?"

To have you depart, Alastair thought. Aloud, he said, "Kittredge and I were to play brag."

"Ah, I am not the best at that game, but shall we play a few rounds while we wait for your friend's return? I will endeavor my best to give you some measure of challenge."

As he was not interested in encouraging conversation with the man, Alastair started shuffling the cards.

"What is the ante?"

"You wish to bet?"

"Cards are hardly fun if nothing is at stake."

"Name your bet then."

Devon straightened, perhaps not wanting to name an amount too low for fear of appearing miserly or cowardly, nor too high to risk losing. "Will five guineas be sufficient?"

"If it pleases you."

His indifferent response appeared to disappoint the Viscount. Alastair dealt three cards each.

"Have you been back to Château Follet since last we met?" Devon asked as he looked at his cards.

"I have not," Alastair replied blandly.

"Nor have I."

"Place your bet."

"Ah, well, let me add another five guineas then."

Alastair matched the bet.

"But I should like to return before long," Devon continued, his brow furrowing as he pondered whether to bet again or fold. "I did not have the chance to inquire if Miss Abbey—your cousin, is she not?—had enjoyed her stay at Château Follet?"

Alastair clenched his jaw.

"She is a charming creature. How marvelous that you hail from the same family. It was quite the coincidence that you should both be there at the same time."

"You may double the pot if you wish to see the cards."

"Ah, yes, perhaps I shall. That would make it another twenty guineas then."

"Forty."

"Forty it is."

Alastair laid down his cards, a run that edged out Devon's flush.

"I forgot how quickly this game finishes," Devon said as Alastair presented Devon with the cards to shuffle.

After a new pot had been established and the cards dealt, Devon asked, "Will Miss Abbey be returning to Follet?"

"No," Alastair answered quickly.

Devon's brows rose. "No? I pray she was not disappointed in Follet?"

"Her attendance at the château was a rare occasion, and she will not be returning."

"You are in communication with her then? She has confided this to you?"

"You take an interest in Miss Abbey?"

"As you are her cousin, I will admit to you that I found her rather captivating. Say again the reason she will not be returning to Follet?"

"I had not provided a reason."

"If she does not plan on returning, I can only hazard that she had a disappointing experience, and that is a travesty, for no one ought leave Château Follet unsatisfied."

Alastair was tempted to say that she had been more than

satisfied with her experience but kept his mouth shut except to say, "Your bet, sir."

"Where does Miss Abbey hail from?"

"Why do you wish to know?"

Devon turned his study from his cards to Alastair. "It would seem you are protective of her."

She needs protecting from wolves like you, Alastair thought. "As you are a frequent guest at the Château Follet, you must be aware that discretion is the value most honored."

Devon placed a bet of five guineas and said, "I am more than aware, and during my tenure at Château Follet, I have never once divulged or let slip any indiscretion."

Alastair put in another five. Devon contemplated before doing the same.

"I think I would like the pleasure of seeing Miss Abbey again."

"Do you?"

"Indeed, I thought I might be able to find her here in town."

Alastair felt his body tighten. "I find your interest in her surprising, for she is hardly the most captivating maiden."

"I am not so shallow that a pretty countenance is all that matters to me. While Miss Abbey may not be a beauty in the ordinary sense of the word, I can see she has other lovely qualities to recommend her."

"Such as?" Alastair asked, managing not to grit his teeth.

Devon leaned in. "I suspect, as a fellow guest of Madame Follet, you understand what these qualities are."

"I think my preferences differ from yours."

"They cannot be two different or we would not both find ourselves at Château Follet."

"You had the company of Miss Abbey for but a small amount of time, hardly enough to form a substantive impression of her qualities."

"*Au contraire*, I am quite good at making an assessment in a short amount of time."

Alastair would have liked nothing more than to have Devon lose a sum sizable enough to compel his departure, but he held a poor hand. "I will see your cards."

Devon also held only a high card, but his queen of diamonds beat Alastair's jack of spades.

"Shall we up the ante to augment the excitement?" Devon asked, handing Alastair the deck. "Say, ten guineas?"

"As you wish."

After placing their ante, Alastair shuffled and dealt the cards.

"I wish I had had more time with Miss Abbey. I wondered how she had spent the remainder of the evening at Château Follet."

"She arrived at Château Follet in error. I kept watch over her till I could see her safely departed in the morning."

"Then she did not have a chance to partake of the château's offerings."

"As I said, she came in error," Alastair said without looking up from his cards, a pair of threes.

Devon placed ten guineas for his bet. "She seemed quite at ease with the activities of the château—and eager to participate."

"Nevertheless, her time with Château Follet is done."

"You are her guardian?"

"I am not—"

"Then how can you be certain?"

Alastair put in ten guineas. "I think your efforts would be better spent attending to other ladies."

"Miss Abbey intrigues me."

"She would not suit your preferences."

"You presume to know me, my lord?"

There was a slight edge in his tone, but Alastair cared little if he should offend the man.

"I have heard of your preferences from my friend, the Baron Rockwell."

Devon frowned at this. "I mean no disregard to your friend, but Rockwell makes a great many presumptions. He is not always right."

"Do you deny you are partial to virgins?"

Devon put in twenty guineas before responding with lifted chin, "I do not. Virgins are delightful, and I consider it an honor to introduce them to the pleasures of the flesh. When you say that Miss Abbey would not suit me, do you mean to say that she is not a virgin?"

"I mean to say that you will stay away from Miss Abbey," Alastair glowered.

"That has the ring of a threat, my lord."

"Then consider it a threat." Alastair folded his cards. "Our game is at an end, sir."

Devon smirked as he displayed his cards, surprising Alastair. He held only an eight for a high card. "It would seem I am better at brag than I thought. I suppose I ought not be underestimated."

He collected his winnings. "I would have provided Miss Abbey an unforgettable experience at Château Follet. It is unfortunate I had not the opportunity to do so. But…perhaps another time."

"You will deem me more presumptuous than Rockwell, but I doubt you are up to the task of satisfying Miss Abbey's expectations." Alastair had the satisfaction of seeing Devon's nostrils flare. "Take care you do not *over*estimate your appeal."

"Your cousin found me appealing enough. Had you not intervened, she would have—"

Alastair had risen, prompting Devon to rise to his feet as well. The two men regarded each other tensely till Kittredge appeared, holding a decanter of wine. "Your pardon. I had not intended to take long…"

"Thank you for the play," Devon said without taking his eyes off Alastair. "And the winnings."

With a bow, the Viscount took his leave.

"What the bloody hell happened?" Kittredge asked Alastair when Devon had left. "You look ready to pummel the man."

Alastair sat back down. "You took a damned long time looking for Thistlewood."

"Found him in the cellar. He wanted my opinion on some Madeira. What the devil happened between you and this Viscount? Did he cheat at cards?"

"No, though I would not put it past him to do so," Alastair answered as he watched Devon across the room.

Kittredge sat down and filled two glasses with wine. "Hm. Then I can't imagine what he could have done to earn your ire. Did he criticize your family? No, that would not trouble you. Is he your competition for the Lady Sophia?"

Alastair turned to his friend.

"He is a handsome fellow, to be sure," Kittredge continued, "but you outrank him, and that is no small matter for the daughter of a duke. The betting book at Brooks's has you in the lead for the fair damsel's hand, though there are just as many bets that you will not marry for at least another five years."

Taking the glass of wine from Kittredge, Alastair drank it without tasting the port. Though he had paid more attention to the woman, Lady Sophia, than was his custom, his mind dwelt at present upon Millie. If Devon knew she was his cousin, he could easily discern that Miss Abbey was none other than Miss Abbott.

"Is that not a fine port?" Kittredge asked, refilling his own glass before it was even done. "I say we drink of it as much as we can and sleep well past the noon hour before we depart for the hunting grounds of Suffolk."

"The grounds at Edenmoor are good for hunting this time of year," Alastair thought aloud.

"Eh?"

"My aunt's estate."

"Not sure your aunt would be pleased to have my company, as she thinks I encourage your vices, but do as you please, Alastair. I will go wherever a good glass of wine can be had."

CHAPTER EIGHT

---◇◆◇◆◇---

NOT HAVING SEEN KATHERINE SINCE their trip to Bath, Mildred was overjoyed to see her ladyship. Katherine took her hand in her own and pressed it warmly in reception. Mildred could hardly wait to have a moment alone with the woman.

"You are a welcome sight to these old eyes," Katherine said, taking Mildred's arm in hers, as she led the Abbotts into her house.

"You may describe your eyes as old, but they are sharper than mine," Mildred replied. She never regarded her ladyship as old, despite the appearance of grey in her hair and wrinkles at the corners of her eyes and mouth. Her ladyship was still possessed of impeccable posture and a stout carriage.

"I regret that it has been so long since last we had each other's company, but Harriett required me."

Harriett was Lady Katherine's daughter by her first husband.

"I pray she is in better health?" Mildred asked.

They had a moment of partial solitude, for her father, still drowsy from his nap, walked at a slow pace behind them. Her mother would have been at their side but was busy marveling at her surroundings.

"Yes, but I forbid her to make the trip to Edenmoor till the babe is older."

"You must be overjoyed to have another grandson."

Katherine beamed. "He is quite the rumbustious little babe, as are all the d'Aubigne men."

Mrs. Abbott came up to them. "What a fine entry you have, Lady Katherine! What brightness fills this space! And how nicely appointed all your furnishings and decor are. So light and uplifting to the mood!"

"I must credit Richard for that. My first husband was partial to dark hues, and as all our furniture was made of mahogany then, it all felt rather somber. I pray you will make yourselves comfortable here. You are first arrived and have the run of the place."

"And whom else shall we be delighted to expect?"

"My son, Edward, his wife and sons will arrive today. My nieces, Louisa and Caroline, will come the day before Michaelmas and stay two days."

"What? We shall have the pleasure of their company but two days? It is quite the distance to travel for such a short duration."

"The distance is nothing for the young," Mildred intervened, though her mother's lack of grace had never seemed to bother Katherine. Mildred was secretly relieved that Louisa Wilmington and Caroline Brewster would not stay for the entire sennight. She had met the women sparingly, but neither could hide their disdain that Katherine had chosen a second husband so far beneath her station.

"And when does your nephew arrive?" Mrs. Abbott asked of Katherine.

Mildred stiffened.

"I do not expect him at all," Katherine answered.

"Indeed? He will not spend Michaelmas with his family?"

"Alastair does as Alastair pleases."

Still unsatisfied, Mrs. Abbott inquired, "I hope he is well?"

"I have no reason to believe otherwise. He did not elaborate in his letter to me."

Mrs. Abbott raised her brows. "Oh?"

"Come, Mother, let us see to our chambers," Mildred said.

As they proceeded through the house, Mrs. Abbott had the grandeur of the staircase, the warm and engaging tapestries in the hall, and the very fine paintings upon the walls to distract her. After leaving Mr. and Mrs. Abbott in their chambers, Katherine showed Mildred to her own room. With a window that overlooked the gardens and pastel silk upon the walls, the room was delightful to Mildred.

"I shall have tea ready within the hour," Katherine said, "and hope that is enough time for you to change out of your traveling clothes."

Mildred nodded. "I cannot thank you enough for your invitation to spend Michaelmas with your family. My mother was beyond thrilled, and I think her excitement overwhelms her..."

"Do not fret of that, my dear. While I understand why Richard was hesitant to have me consort with your family, I had told him it troubled me little. I may be a d'Aubigne, but *you* know that I am not a conventional sort of woman."

The women shared a smile.

"I shall be forever grateful to have had your acquaintance, my lady," Mildred said.

"I require none of your sentimentality, my girl, but I will find a moment for the two of us. I wish to hear how you have fared all this time."

With the appearance of the dressing maid, Lady Katherine took her leave. As Mildred divested her coat, she recalled that the Marquess was not to spend Michaelmas at Edenmoor. She could not help but be a little disappointed, as their last exchange had been unsatisfactory. But she was also relieved that he was to be absent. Though she was determined to maintain their relationship as it had been prior to Château

Follet, she knew she would be deceiving herself that it could be perfectly the same.

"ARE YOU DISAPPOINTED?" LADY KATHERINE asked.

Her ladyship and Mildred strolled the manor after tea. Mrs. Abbott, fatigued from the traveling, had retired to her chambers to rest. Mr. Abbott read the newspaper in the sunroom.

"Disappointed?" Mildred echoed.

"That he will not be here."

"How could I be when I have your company?" Mildred cried.

Katherine smiled. "Nonetheless, you would rather he were joining us."

Mildred shook her head. "For what purpose would I desire to see him? He refused my request to return my dowry to its initial amount, and it is too late now for him to change his mind."

"There need not be a *purpose*. If you take pleasure in seeing him, that stands irrespective of anything else."

Mildred studied her ladyship, wondering if the woman had attempted, as she had with the Château Follet, to put the two of them in each other's way once more? But there could be no reason for a second meeting. Mildred would be forever grateful to Lady Katherine for her introduction to Château Follet, and grateful that she had set it up so that Alastair could be the one to fulfill her desired night of debauchery. Her ladyship knew that if she had revealed her plans to Mildred, Mildred would have balked at the notion of submitting herself to the Marquess.

"My vexation with him has not vanished," Mildred said.

"I have been besieged by all manner of unwanted suitors, and my present misery is all due to Alastair."

"Is there none among them that you would consider for a husband?"

Mildred shuddered, but then she considered Mr. Winston. She wondered what sort of husband he might make.

"Ah, there is one," her ladyship discerned. "Who is he?"

"His name is George Winston."

"That name is vaguely familiar, but I do not think I have the pleasure of knowing this man."

"I mention him only because he is more tolerable than the others. His manners are pleasing, and he is both intelligent and articulate."

"That sounds quite promising. Do your parents approve of him?"

"He has a gentleman's income, undoubtedly, but my mother believes there are better prospects to be had. But I am inspired by you, my lady, to place more weight upon the character of a spouse than his riches."

"I did come under much criticism when I married Richard, but then, I had done my duty in my first marriage, and as my children were settled in their marriages, I had more freedom to follow my heart."

Mildred looked out the window. How her life would differ if she had a similar liberty.

"I had thought I would sooner be a spinster than wed a man I did not love or desire," she remarked. "But it is my duty, and I should be considered most ungrateful if I did not choose to marry. Many young women have not the privileges I now have."

"Then be ungrateful. I should hate to see your spirit crushed by the weight of an unhappy marriage."

"There is not a man who could accommodate me, and the fault is entirely my own I fear I am too fastidious…and too wicked."

"Do not give up hope, my dear. Come, let me show you something."

Lady Katherine led her to the end of the corridor, produced a key, and unlocked a set of double doors. They entered a room of darkness, but her ladyship found the curtains covering the room's lone window and drew them aside.

Though the rest of the house was light and airy, this room was dark and could appear, without light, foreboding, with its dark wood paneling, bare flooring and stone hearth. Mildred's breath stalled as she gazed about the room. Many of the apparatuses were familiar to her—as she had seen them at Château Follet.

Heat percolated in her loins as she beheld a Saint Andrew's cross and remembered what it had been like to be shackled to one. She observed a wooden bench that was meant to be straddled, for the back of the bench was on the narrow side. Beside the bench stood a pillory. It was slightly above waist height, and she did not think she would be very comfortable locked in one of those.

"You have your own Château Follet," Mildred noted with awe and even envy.

"Given that Richard and I shared this interest, it was much more practical to have our own place. Traveling to Château Follet is difficult in winter, and we often had not the patience to make the journey."

Mildred looked about the room once more. She would consider herself truly blessed if she should find a man as Lady Katherine had.

"The room gets dusty from want of use," her ladyship said, "but I clean it from time to time, as the servants do not enter. I will not let it fall into disrepair, as it holds too many memories for me."

"You have many fine rooms, my lady," Mildred remarked, "but this one is my favorite."

CHAPTER NINE

"AND HOW LONG DO YOU intend we stay at Eden-moor?" Kittredge asked as he and Alastair rode on horseback toward Katherine's estate.

"Not more than two days and a night, I think," replied Alastair, who preferred riding over the bumping and jarring of a carriage. The confinement did not suit his temperament, and the autumn air pacified the agitation that had come upon him ever since his encounter with Devon.

"What? All this way for but two days?"

Alastair thought of his sisters and shuddered inside. Katherine's son would be there as well with his family. He did not mind Edward as much but still he had no desire to make conversation with him or his wife, Anne. Their young sons, aged six to twelve, could be quarrelsome with each other and far too boisterous for his taste. He did not think his cousin Harriett and her family would be present, and Mr. and Mrs. Abbott were too intimidated by him to require much of his attention. Nonetheless, he wondered that he could tolerate even two days in such company.

"Is the hunting that superb?" Kittredge inquired.

"It is more than adequate."

"Then say again why we are headed there?"

"I did not say before, but you may content yourself that my aunt keeps a decent cellar."

"Will your niece, Emily, be there? She had her come out last year, did she not? She is quite the tempting armful."

Alastair returned a stern gaze.

"Worry not," Kittredge laughed. "I have no designs upon your family. I prefer you as friend and not kin. Good God, I should hate to have you for a brother-in-law. Will your uncle be there?"

"Traveling aggravates his joints."

"I do like Herbert. And his clarets even more."

Alastair could not bear the company of Katherine's brother any more than he cared for the company of his sisters, whom he would now have to suffer for at least a full day.

He cursed himself. Selecting Millie to fulfill Katherine's birthday request had become a much greater task than he had ever envisioned. He could have waited till Millie returned to London to speak to her, but he worried what Katherine might say or do. He would never have guessed that his aunt would take Millie to the Château Follet, though she had orchestrated the coincidence well. Who knew what other absurdity the two women might attempt?

Having discovered that Millie harbored such wanton and dark desires, he understood why Katherine, who had introduced him to Follet, had brought Millie there. Nevertheless, it was a risky proposition and remained so. He doubted Millie could handle herself with the likes of Devon. He could not chance Millie returning to Château Follet, and he would not now be surprised if Katherine would encourage just such a thing.

"Well! This is a most welcome surprise!" his aunt exclaimed when they had arrived at Edenmoor.

"I pray you had received the notice of our coming?" Alastair asked.

"I did, and have prepared rooms for you, though your notice only said that you *might* come. Where are your valets and baggage?"

"Not far behind. You remember Kittredge."

His friend doffed his hat and bowed.

"I do," Katherine responded. She put aside her reservations. "Welcome, good sir."

"Are my sisters arrived?"

"They come tomorrow, but Edward is here with his family. And the Abbotts." To Kittredge, she explained, "They are relations of my late husband, Richard."

"I look forward to making their acquaintance," Kittredge said.

Alastair looked about, expecting to see the Cheswith boys tearing through the halls. "Where is everyone?"

"Millie is out back playing with the boys."

He found it interesting that she had responded with regards to the one person he had come to see. His gaze came to rest upon a large painting of Richard and Katherine from some years ago. The two had met at Château Follet and fallen in love there. Alastair hoped that was not what Katherine expected for Millie.

Feeling the study of his aunt, he turned to her. "Kittredge and I will greet the others after we have changed out of our riding clothes."

"Let me show you to your rooms then."

She could have had a servant see them to their rooms, but Alastair suspected she offered so that she could speak with him. And he was correct. After seeing Kittredge settled, she walked Alastair down the corridor.

"What prompted your decision to join us for Michaelmas?" she asked.

He had anticipated this question and had no reservations about being candid with her. "Millie."

Katherine's countenance brightened.

"I came across a rogue, one she became acquainted with

while at Follet, and I mean to warn the both of you that he may seek her out."

She frowned. "That is against the etiquette of Château Follet."

"He is quite taken with Millie."

"That is hardly a surprise."

"For reasons you should find troubling. He thinks her a virgin." He turned to face her. "I hope you do not entertain any notions of returning Millie to Château Follet."

"I had not considered it."

"I pray you do not."

"Why not?"

"I cannot always be there to protect her against unsavory characters."

Katherine beamed. "How grand that you take such an interest in her welfare."

"Madam, I bid you consider the matter with seriousness. Do *not* take Millie back to Château Follet."

"Andre, if she desires to return, why should I not facilitate her happiness?"

"Has she expressed a desire to return?"

"Not explicitly. We have not been in each other's company of late, and I hope she and I will have more occasion to speak now."

"You ought to discourage any thoughts of returning."

Katherine sighed.

"You are partial to Millie," he continued, "and if *you* care for her, you will want to see her unharmed. You cannot let your affections for Château Follet cloud your judgment. I bid you be the responsible party."

"Of course I would not wish to place her in harm's way, and because I esteem your display of consideration for another human being, I will honor your request."

He turned to enter his room, but he was only partially

satisfied. He would not wager all that he had that Katherine would do exactly as he wanted. And there was also the matter of Millie. He would not be wholly surprised if she dared return to Château Follet without Katherine's participation.

MILLIE WAS WRONG. THOUGH SHE had protested that the nature of their relationship would not change, it had.

Dressed in fresh clothing, Alastair found her outside playing Blind Man's Bluff with the Cheswith boys and a few servants' children. Millie had the blindfold, and the children scurried around, laughing and calling out to her. Alastair watched for several minutes, but when he saw her headed toward a pit in the ground, he strode over. He was too far to reach her in time, and she seemed not to hear him call out her name. She stumbled to her knees, but he caught her before she tripped on her own skirts in her attempt to rise.

It felt pleasing to hold her.

When he had righted her, she lifted the blindfold, saying, "Goodness, I had not—"

Upon seeing him, her face reddened. She had rarely blushed with him before. He released her with some reluctance.

"M-My lord," she greeted, "you—you're here."

He saw that she had on a much nicer bonnet than he had seen her in last. It suited her.

"Lady Katherine had not said…"

"I had not confirmed my coming with her," he explained.

She seemed to collect herself. "Your presence must please your family greatly."

He wanted to ask it if pleased *her,* but he could ascertain this soon enough. The children complained about the stall. She glanced at her dirt-covered skirts. brushing them off.

He addressed the eldest Cheswith boy. "Thomas, take Miss Abbott's place so that she can tend to her gown."

"That won't be necessary," Millie said. "I can continue. 'Tis but a little dust."

He took the blindfold from her and gave it to Thomas. To Millie, he said, "I will walk you to the house."

"Truly, I am not injured."

He raised a brow. She gave a sigh as if relenting to a persistent child and walked with him. They were silent at first, before he asked, "You do not intend to ask why I am here?"

"Are you inviting me to pry?" she returned with a grin.

"No, but most would be curious to understand my motives."

"You do as you please. It is not my place to question or judge your motives."

He wondered if her reasons were because she knew that he preferred not to be questioned or because she was indifferent to what his answer might be.

"And most would inquire as to how you found the roads, or how your hunting fared," she observed, "but you would disdain these sorts of *tete-a-tetes*."

"You know me well, Millie."

She smiled. "You are not complicated, my lord."

"Nevertheless, I find most people unable to refrain from their own inclinations, regardless of my preferences."

"Does it trouble you that others do not always grant you what you want?"

"As the only son of a marquess, I have been quite spoilt and accustomed to receiving what I want."

She chuckled. "Yes, you are."

He stopped. "I did not seek your agreement of my statement."

"No, but you have it. As I do not think we often agree on anything, I thought it a special occasion to take note of."

He shook his head. His cousin could easily earn both his approbation and his vexation. He wanted to forbid her return to Château Follet, but she would balk at such an arrogant attempt to control her. They resumed walking.

"Whilst in town, I came across your friend, the Viscount Devon," he said.

"Indeed?"

He frowned at her apparent interest. "He is not a man worth your attention, Millie."

"So you have said before."

"I would stay your distance from him."

"I doubt my path will cross with his."

"But if it should, you will heed my cautions?"

She studied him before replying, "You need not worry that I shall lift my skirts upon meeting him."

"And what if he should attempt to seduce you?"

She seemed amused by the idea. "I am certain there are far better conquests for him."

"You need not demean yourself so. You have many qualities to recommend you."

This time, she stopped and looked at him. There was a brightness to her eyes he found quite fetching.

"You are kind, my lord," she said.

He was about to decry being fixed with the trait when Kittredge appeared.

"There you are, Alastair. I have reviewed your aunt's cellar—"

Upon seeing Millie, he bowed. Alastair made the necessary introductions. After a brief dialogue of politeness between Millie and Kittredge, Millie said that she would head to her room.

Alastair had little opportunity to speak alone with Millie, for Edward engaged him next with details of a hunt for the following morning. He could not speak to her during dinner, and she made no effort to seek his company afterward. Quite the contrary, she seemed to stay her distance from him, choosing to speak with Anne mostly. He did see her glance his way, however, when she thought he wasn't looking.

When Anne and the Abbotts chose to retire for the evening, Millie said she would do the same. Alastair stayed with Edward and Kittredge till the two men had had their fill of sherry and port. In his chambers, Alastair remained awake, considering how he could speak with Millie in private before or after the hunt.

But he need not have waited till the morrow. An hour after everyone had gone to bed, he heard footsteps pass his chambers. Even before he opened his door, he suspected it was Millie.

CHAPTER TEN

MILDRED WANTED ANOTHER LOOK AT the room of wicked debauchery. She had not seen Lady Katherine lock the room after showing it to her upon the first day, and when she tried the doors, she found they indeed opened.

She closed the door behind her and, using her own candle, lit a candelabra. She took in a long breath as she gazed about the room a second time. Passing the pillory, she went to the sideboard, above which hung two canes, three floggers, and a crop. She picked up the heaviest of the floggers, wondering how heavy a blow the wide leather straps would deal and if she could withstand them?

Replacing the flogger, she opened one of the drawers of the sideboard and found a collar; a pair of clamps; two hollow glass tube, with tops akin to a surgeon's syringe; several metal rings, each smaller than the tip of a finger; and two tiny pairs of half-spheres joined together. The clamps she remembered well. Alastair had applied a similar pair to her nipples. She remembered the pinching pain, a lovely, exquisite sensation that wakened her whole body. Her nipples hardened at the memory, and she passed her hand over her bosom to calm the quickening heartbeat.

The middle drawer contained items of equal puzzlement. She picked up a glass object shaped like an elongated teardrop but with a wide base. Setting it down, she looked next at a series of beads connected by a string, and then another glass teardrop, this one with a fox tail attached to the end. Intrigued, she wished she could ask what these were for. Perhaps she would work up the nerve to ask Katherine.

The third and final drawer made her gasp.

Nestled atop silk lining were several dildos of varying size. She picked up one made of glass and admired its smooth finish. The craftsmanship was rather impressive, for the crafter had shaped the top to resemble the flare at the tip of a cock. Laying down the glass dildo, she picked up a smaller wooden one with ridges. She wondered that such a hard object could render pleasure, for a true cock, though hard, had some softness to it. The third and final dildo was made of a material resembling India rubber. It was quite large both in length and girth. She shuddered to think of her cunnie swallowing such a large object. Nevertheless, she picked it up to marvel at its size and instinctively licked her lips. She remembered how delicious Alastair's cock had tasted.

Looking at the cock she held, she wondered if she could wrap her mouth about this monstrosity. Feeling mischievous, she put the dildo to her mouth. She licked its tip, then pushed it between her lips. She took in two inches and felt her lips stretch over the circumference. Desire swirled in her groin. How she wished she had a real cock to hold!

"Now *that* is a sight worth four thousand pounds."

In her haste to pull the dildo out, she bobbled it several times before dropping it altogether. She felt herself flushing to the roots of her hair. But was somewhat relieved to see it was Alastair at the threshold. How long had he been standing there? Despite the late hour, he still wore his clothes but had his banyan instead of his coat.

"I wondered if Katherine had told you of this room," he said.

She bent down to pick up the dildo. After brushing it off

with her robe, she intended to return it to the drawer.

"Not yet," he bid as he walked into the room. "I interrupted your feasting."

Her blushed deepened. "I was merely...it is of such a ridiculous width, I merely wondered..."

"How much of it you could swallow?" He stood in front of her and cupped the hand that held the dildo. "Let us find out"

Her heart drummed in her ears as she allowed his hands to guide the dildo back to her mouth. She parted her lips and relaxed her tongue to permit the behemoth entry. She could take no more than three inches before gagging.

"A little more," he encouraged.

Wanting to please him of a sudden, she did her best to take in more. Her mouth was stretched to capacity, and though she took in air through her nose, breathing felt awkward whilst her mouth was stuffed by the false cock. She gazed up at him and the molten lust in his eyes made her throb between the legs. She would stand with her mouth stuffed by cock for hours, mesmerized by the expression of desire in his countenance. It satisfied her to know that he was not immune to her.

"You may release it," he said, drawing the hand with the dildo back down.

She licked her lips and waited to see what he would do next. Did she dare hope he would stay? Releasing her hands, he took a step back. He would now advise her to return to her chambers, she predicted with disappointment. It would be of no use. She could not sleep, not after seeing all that she had, not after he had witnessed her partaking of a false cock. Her hands still felt warm from his touch.

"It is hard to imagine her ladyship making use of such implements," she said when she could no longer bear the silence. "Or do you think they are merely for show?"

"My aunt and I do not discuss the particulars of what she and Richard did behind closed doors."

Mildred nodded. Perhaps it was best not to imagine her ladyship engaged in wicked wantonness. She put the large dildo back in its place. Realizing that Alastair would be familiar with the possessions in the room, she steadied the flutters inside of her and asked, "Would you indulge my curiosity?"

He crossed his arms. "No."

"Why not?"

"Because I am not inclined."

"Really, Alastair! You can be quite selfish."

"Only 'quite' selfish? I must be softening in my old age."

Her lower lip dropped for a moment, but then she saw a small glimmer in his eyes and resolved that she would not permit him to rile her.

"At the gaming hall, you had threatened to shower me with praises for my *generosity*," he reminded her.

"Yes, and I did write you several letters to that effect. You responded to none of them."

"I grew wearing of receiving them."

"You could have put an end to them if you but acquiesced to my request."

By saying nothing, he seemed to acknowledge her point.

"I merely wondered as to the purpose of a few items," she explained, opening the first drawer once more. She picked up the set of tiny half spheres stuck together. "These, for instance."

"Katherine encourages your pursuit in such matters. Why do you not ask her?"

"Because she is asleep. And you are…here."

In the dim and flickering light, she thought she saw a corner of his lips turn upward. "I will answer *one* question."

"You refused a far more significant request of mine."

"And because of that I am to grant all other requests of yours?"

"Why do you persist in being difficult? Does it amuse you to trifle with me?"

"The answer to your latter question is yes. As to the former, I will not encourage your prurience."

"Encourage my—" She gasped. "You had me take that— that ridiculously large cock into my mouth!"

His smile reached both corners of his lips this time.

"How is that not encouraging my prurience?" she threw at him.

"I am at ease with my hypocrisy. If it unsettles *you*—"

She scowled. "You deserve to be turned over the knee and walloped."

"Undoubtedly. Fortunately, I never assume the role of submission."

His mention of the part she had played at Château Follet made her backside tingle with the memory of how he had applied the crop to her rump.

"Very well," she said, putting the spheres back, "but I shall divine the uses of these curious objects, if not from Katherine, then…"

He drew a step closer, and all humor had left his tone. "Then what?"

"Perhaps another visit to the Château Follet will—"

He grasped her arm and turned her to him. "You are not returning to the château."

His pronouncement nettled her. "Why not?"

"You have been there already."

"That is no answer at all. There is no reason I should not return there if I wish. And I would favor another visit."

"No reason? You would risk your honor, your family?"

"We have had this discussion before, Alastair."

She attempted to withdraw her arm, but he did not let her

go.

"And even if I am ruined," she continued, "I still have a dowry of four thousand pounds for an incentive."

"The sort of man willing to take a compromised woman for four thousand pounds is not the sort of man you wish to marry."

"In truth, I have no wish to marry at all, but *you* and my parents have thrust the matter upon me."

"I will not accompany you to Château Follet."

"I did not expect you would. I certainly would not ask you to."

This seemed to startle him. "Then how—did Katherine offer to take you there?"

"No, she need not, but if I wrote to Madame Follet, I do not think she would deny me an invitation."

"And who would serve as your partner? Who would play the dominant to your submissive?"

"If you recall, a partner is not required. I can find someone there. And had you not intervened the last time, I might have found myself with the Viscount Devon."

She saw the vein at his temple throb and wondered if she ought not have mentioned Devon.

"You are bloody lucky you escaped his clutches," Alastair growled, his grip on her arm tightening. "I'll be damned if you let my prior efforts go to waste with that bleeder."

"Then satisfy my curiosity! Really, Alastair. I wonder at your sense sometimes."

A muscle along his jaw rippled, but he let her go. "*One* question, Millie. The hour is late."

She rolled her eyes, which she saw raised his ire. She watched him grab the spheres.

"These," he said, opening his hand, "are magnets and operate similar to clamps."

Intrigued, she peered into his palm at the small, shiny

objects. How she dearly wished to have these affixed to her nipples! She felt a familiar ache between her legs.

"If I am in a decent mood tomorrow, you may ask a second question," Alastair said before turning to put the spheres back.

"But that was not my question," she protested. "If I am allotted but one question tonight, it would be this…will you be my dominant?"

CHAPTER ELEVEN

"HAVE YOU NO RESTRAINT, WOMAN?" Alastair returned, trying to ignore the tension in his groin. His cock had already stretched when he saw those lovely lips encasing the large dildo.

She lifted her chin and spoke as if she had proposed nothing more than a game of whist. "I thought it was convenient, as I was here, you are here, and there is this room and its accoutrements. It is much more expedient than traveling to Château Follet."

He thought of the Viscount Devon. Once again his cousin had him against a wall, inspiring within him both resentment and awe.

"Millie," he warned.

"What do you care if you encourage my prurience?"

She had challenged him on this before, and he could provide no truly satisfactory response.

"As you are not being reasonable," he replied, "I am obliged to take that role."

"Reasonable? Is offering four thousand pounds for a dowry to a poor relation reasonable?"

"That has nothing to do with here and now."

"You are an odd one, Alastair. I think I liked you better when you were trying not to be reasonable. Your attempts to be good are rather trying."

He could not resist smiling.

"In truth," she contemplated, "it matters not what you do. Whether you encourage me or not, these wicked desires persist inside me. If I am to be shackled by matrimony in the near future, I will indulge my prurience while I can. I asked for your assistance, but if you will not provide it, I will find other ways to address my needs."

He did not doubt that she would.

"Very well, I shall grant this request of yours, and it shall be the last request I ever grant you. On one condition: you promise never to return to Château Follet."

In silence, she weighed his proposition before saying, "I want an experience as fulfilling as that which would occur at Château Follet. You will answer every curiosity of mine, indulge every whim, attend to every desire?"

He groaned as heat churned in his loins. "If you behave yourself."

She nodded. "If I do not, you may punish me as you see fit. We may renew our arrangement as it was at Château Follet."

Blood surged through his cock. There was no turning back now, no matter how strongly his mind might be bent against it. "Do you recall your word of safety?"

When she could not, he supplied it for her. "Pearls."

"I should like to begin with these little curiosities," she said, reaching for the half spheres.

He closed his hand before she could take them. "I want your word, Millie."

"I promise not to return to Château Follet."

Satisfied, he opened his hand and pried the sphere in twain. "These magnets are strong. They will be worse than the clamps."

Her eyes widened, but she was not daunted. She took the magnets and joined them together. "May I try them? My lord."

A series of curses ran through his head.

He pushed aside the lapels of her robe and loosened the strings of her shift. With a crooked finger, he tugged the décolletage down. Her bosom rose as she inhaled. His knuckle brushed against the softness of her breast as he drew the shift down toward her nipple. The rosebud was already taught with anticipation. He nudged it before trapping it between his thumb and forefinger. He pulled gently. Her back arched subtly, sending her bosom closer to him. He rolled and flicked the nipple, slowly, teasingly, still her breath grew shorter. He pinched the nub, harder and harder, till she yelped. He released it and repeated the treatment on her other nipple. He pinched and twisted this one. She squirmed, not from pain, but from her arousal.

"May I try these now, my lord?" She lifted her hand with the magnets.

"Not yet." He needed to ensure that her level of arousal was high enough for her to tolerate the pain. He loosened the sash of her robe and cupped her mons. She gasped in surprise.

"Are you wet?"

"A little, I think."

His hand nestled farther between her thighs. Her dampness began to seep through the fabric to his fingers. She was more than a little wet. He rubbed her shift into her, making her moan. He watched as her lashes fluttered, her breath became uneven, and her mouth remained open, inviting him to kiss her, to force his tongue down into that lovely orifice.

"Do you remember my rules?"

"To address you always as 'my lord.'"

"And?"

"Require your permission to spend."

"Good."

She closed her eyes as he intensified his fondling. His fingers pressed the damp undergarment into her folds, grazing her clitoris. Her every reaction called to the primal in him, from the breaths that filled his ears to the scent of her arousal wafting through his nose. When he sensed she was ready, he took the magnets from her hand, reached beneath her shift and placed a half sphere on either side of her right nipple.

She gave a sharp cry, both hands grabbing his wrist, when he allowed the magnets to adhere to each other.

"Breathe long and slow," he recommended.

She did as he bid, and he allowed her grasp to tighten about him.

"Do you require your safety word?" he asked.

She breathed out through her mouth, and after a long pause, shook her head. He took her left hand and placed it between her legs.

"Stroke yourself."

While she complied, he released her other hand from him and pulled the right side of her robe down her shoulder. The right side of the shift followed, baring the breast now adorned with the magnets. He stepped back to admire the jewelry pinching her nipple and had to adjust his crotch. Should he allow her to spend, the more magnanimous part of him wondered?

No. She had not made it easy for him, and he would return the favor. She needed to appreciate the challenges present at Château Follet. The Viscount Devon would have shown her no mercy, and Alastair intended to cast away any chance that she might reconsider her promise to him.

For several minutes he watched her pleasure herself. "Do you wish to spend?"

She nodded. "Please, my lord."

"We should apply the other pair."

He sauntered to the sideboard to find the other set of magnets. She braced herself but presented her other breast.

Returning, he slid the left side of her robe off her shoulder, then pulled down the strap of the shift. He eyed her left breast in appreciation of its shape and paleness of skin. He cradled the orb, relishing the weight, the suppleness in his palm, and brushed his thumb over the already erect nipple. She shuddered. He needed the flesh, gently at first before manhandling it. She purred her preference. He tugged the nipple to ensure it was at its peak before applying the magnets.

She groaned as the little spheres pinched the base of her nipple. Her garments, which had fallen about her hips, slid to the floor. She shivered. Though it was a warmer autumn than in past years, the night air was still cool. A fire had not been lit in the room for many years. Her body would warm soon enough and be distracted by other more urgent sensations.

To cultivate her own heat, he cupped her head in both hands and lowered his mouth to hers. He kissed tenderly, teasing her, for she seemed to prefer a harder application of roughness. His tongue grazed her lips, and though she parted them, he did not dwell inside her mouth but took light mouthfuls of the surface. A small whine grumbled low in her throat.

Relenting, to his own ardor as much as hers, he opened her mouth with his and pushed his tongue between her welcoming lips. He heard her sigh before he muffled her breaths. He probed the hot and wet orifice, crushing her lips so she grunted. Rather than yield, she met the assault upon her, her tongue licking at his as she shoved her mouth to him.

Her fervor took him by surprise. Perhaps time, and the suppression of her lust through it, had intensified her desires. Or perhaps it was the magnets at her nipples that induced the need to release pressure or attention elsewhere. But he liked her passion, liked the duelingof their tongues and the forceful meeting of their mouths. He had a mind to lift her spear himself into her then and there, but he had developed more patience during his time at Château Follet. He knew the benefits of delaying gratification.

He released her and stepped back to view her naked body. Her hair was tied in a plait behind her. Every part of her was exposed. He took her hand and replaced it at her mound. "You may touch yourself."

In silence, he watched her stroke herself for several minutes.

"Do you pleasure yourself at home?"

"Yes."

"How often?"

"It varies, my lord, but, on average, four or five times a week."

Surprised at the frequency, he said, "You are quite the little wanton, Millie."

She blushed. "How often do others of my sex pleasure themselves?"

"In truth, there are some, even those who have been guests at Château Follet, who do not engage in self-pleasure."

"That is sad, my lord, for though it does not afford me the satisfaction of congress, it is better than naught."

"You prefer to have cock?"

Her blush deepened. "I do, my lord."

His cock throbbed at her candor.

"May I ask a question, my lord?"

"You may."

"The other articles in the drawer. What are their purposes?"

He sauntered to the sideboard and inspected the first drawer. He picked up a collar made of leather with metal studs. "The collar denotes ownership. As a submissive, you belong to your dominant. You are his possession. His property. His pet."

She made a face.

Setting down the collar, he walked over to her, pulled the spheres on her right nipple apart before allowing them to snap back together again. She cried out.

"I'll have no show of disrespect, my girl."

"Your pardon, my lord," she murmured.

"A collar must need be earned," he explained, "but because you do not appear fond of it, we will use it to remind you of your status and obligations."

He put the collar about her neck. She looked ravishing in nothing but a collar and little metal spheres adhered to her nipples.

"Thank you, my lord. What of the items in the second drawer?"

He opened the drawer and paused. He would have suspected her a virgin in this third manner of taking cock, but then Millie had a way of surprising him. "These are for penetration of the arse."

"Your pardon?"

"They are inserted into the anus." By her reaction, he deduced that she was still a virgin there. But rather than appear disgusted, she looked intrigued. "This is pleasurable, my lord?"

"Each person is different, but yes, it is intended to be pleasurable."

His cock stretched at the thought of inserting one of the articles into Millie. She closed her eyes, perhaps imagining what it would feel like to have that third hole filled. He noticed her fingers push deeper between her legs.

"May I have your cock, my lord?"

All tension collapsed into the area of his groin. He thought his cock might burst through his pants. He took several deep breaths and would have remained silent had she not opened her eyes and looked at him. Of course he would have liked nothing better than to take possession of her, but she had asked for an experience comparable to one at the Château Follet. There were many experiences to be had there, and they were not all as accommodating as that which he had first provided her.

He would show her the less pleasant aspects of what was expected of a submissive at Château Follet. While she had promised already not to return to Follet, he intended to add further discouragement. It meant he would stay at Eden-moor longer than intended, but he found the prospect not quite as dreadful as expected.

CHAPTER TWELVE

———◈◈◈◈———

"YOU MAY HAVE COCK," ALASTAIR answered slowly before opening the third drawer. "This one."

He held the glass dildo, and Mildred knew not if she were more disappointed that she had been denied his cock or relieved that he had not chosen the monstrosity made of Indian rubber.

"Sit," he beckoned, patting the top of a wooden table.

She slid her derrière onto its surface.

"Farther, that you may have room to place your feet," he instructed.

She did as he bid and bent her legs, bringing her feet onto the top of the table. He spread her knees apart, and, in this lewd position, her quim was fully exposed to him. He slid the length of the smooth glass along her folds. It felt cool to the touch. He rubbed the dildo against her clitoris, swollen from her prior attentions. She was near to spending.

"My lord, may I—"

But he changed the angle of the dildo and pointed its tip at her. He pushed it inside. Her wetness allowed it easy passage. Her cunnie clenched about the unrelenting hardness. He slid more of it into her. At first she found the rigidity of the object awkward, but her arousal reigned supreme, and she soon came to savor the fullness. She would have preferred to be filled by his cock, but the dildo was preferable to nothing.

He nestled the entire length inside her.

"Thank you, my lord," she murmured.

He smiled, and as it was not often that he did so, she felt a sense of accomplishment. He put his thumb to her clitoris, sending flutters through her loins. Gently, he circled the bud, stroking, fondling, wavering it back and forth. The sensation, coupled with the pressure of the dildo inside her, was quite delicious. Despite the discomfort of sitting atop a hard table with her legs indecently spread, she neared spending once more.

But his caresses slowed and he eventually withdrew his hand. "What curiosity would you wish me to address next?"

She wanted to whimper but let out a haggard breath instead. She looked about the room. "Why a pillory?"

"I would think its purpose fairly evident."

"You mean one is actually locked into it?" She knit her brows. "Do you think Uncle Richard or Lady Katherine…?"

"Sometimes the threat of it is sufficient to deter unwanted behavior—or titillate."

Mildred pressed her lips together. The stocks were devices of humiliation and punishment.

"The pillory presents many possibilities," Alastair continued, "as we shall demonstrate."

He assisted her off the table and led her to the device, which differed little from the frameworks that could be seen at Charing Cross or the Haymarket. He lifted the top and gestured for her to take her place. She hesitated but reminded herself that the pillory was to be, as Alastair claimed, titillating, though she wondered, *titillating for whom*? Nonetheless, she placed herself in the frame and allowed him to close the top over her wrists and neck. It was an awkward position, to be bent at the waist, her breasts dangling, her arse protruding. Oddly, she felt her nakedness even more.

"How long am I to remain in this?" she asked

"It depends on my whim, though if you misbehave, I may decide to leave you locked in the pillory all night."

He stood at her side and, reaching below her, cupped a breast. She purred. Her cunnie pulsed. She gasped when he removed the magnets, then screamed when he attached them to a slightly different part of her nipple. He did the same to the other breast. His hands caressed her back and ribs before coming to rest upon her buttocks. He gave one cheek a playful slap before sauntering to the wall that held the canes, floggers, and crops.

"So many choices," he murmured to himself.

Her wetness grew, and she hoped he would reach a decision soon, for she knew she must first suffer the implement of his choice before she would be allowed to spend. She heard him return and stand behind her. She braced herself.

Whack!

From the short, stiff sting, she gathered he had chosen the crop.

"Thank you, my lord."

"You are welcome."

The crop kissed her other cheek with equal vigor. He rained several blows, till her backside grew hot and, she imagined, crimson. He took a respite and reached between her legs to find the moisture trickling down her inner thighs. He caressed her, and that made it all worthwhile. It soothed the burning of her arse. But he was not done.

Withdrawing his hand, he returned to spanking her with the crop. She shifted her weight from one leg to another, partly to relieve the bite of the crop and partly to relieve the discomfort from standing in so awkward a position. She clenched on the dildo, trying to release the pressure inside her. Perhaps if she squeezed hard enough, she could spend.

As if sensing her thoughts on the matter, he removed it, to her dismay. She whimpered at the loss.

"Miss your cock already?"

"Yes, my lord, yes!"

She heard the rustle of clothing and hoped he was unbuttoning his fall to release his cock. Indeed, after a moment, she felt his shaft between her legs, that wonderful veined hardness. He grabbed her hips, slid a length of his cock along her folds. She rejoiced and, casting aside her inhibitions, pushed her derrière at him, her invitation clear. She felt his tip at her opening and could barely contain her glee.

He pulled her onto his shaft. It was more marvelous than the false cock. Slowly, he sank himself farther inside of her, till at last he was buried to the hilt, and she could feel his pants against the backs of her legs and the curls of his hair tickling her buttocks.

She clasped it greedily. There was no finer feeling than that of his erection filling her most intimate parts. She heard him groan as he began to slide himself in and out. Though her legs had begun to grow weary, she now appreciated the angle of his thrusting. His movements were slow, allowing her to savor every inch of him, but she was also impatient for him to increase his pace.

"Thank you, my lord," she said in the hopes of encouraging him. It worked, for he increased his thrusting, his grip tightening on her hips. Beautiful ripples fanned from where he was joined to her. She could feel herself ascending to that rapturous peak. With every effort to bury his cock inside her, his pelvis slapping into her arse, she loved it all, but before she could reach that rapturous summit, he slowed and slid his cock out. She wondered if she had done something wrong. Perhaps she had not thanked him enough.

"I think you're ready to try another object," he said.

Although curious to try something new, she had been happy with his cock inside of her. She heard the drawer to the sideboard open but could not see which drawer. Would he attempt to fit the monstrous dildo inside her now?

After he had returned, she felt an object between her legs. It felt of glass but not as long as the dildo she'd had. He inserted it inside her wetness. It was much smaller than the dildo. He removed it—but she felt it soon enough at another orifice of hers.

Oh dear.

"Do you recall your safety word?"

His question confirmed what was about to happen. He intended to penetrate her arse. She squirmed, unsure that she was ready for or wanted what was to happen.

He slapped her buttock. "Be still."

Whatever he held was small, but when he pressed it at her anus, it felt much larger than it was. Of its own accord, her orifice resisted the intrusion. It was unnatural to have anything *enter* that part of her...

He groped a buttock and gently kneaded the flesh. "Relax."

She nodded and let out a long breath. She felt the tip at her backside once more, stretching her, pressing into her, entering her, then filling her.

The sensation took her breath. How were there so many nerves there?

"Breathe," he reminded her.

Though having the object in her arse was not painful, she considered using her safety word. It was simply too strange and too *full*—and more wanton than she could imagine. Now that the intruder was nestled inside her, her arse seemed content to have it and did not attempt to push it out.

Something tickled her rump, and she jumped, bumping into the pillory that still held her prisoner. Did he brush a plume across her? She attempted to crane her head but could not see past the wooden boards that locked her in place.

He walked toward an apparatus covered by linen, which he yanked off to reveal a looking glass. She saw herself bent at the waist and tried not to fix upon how gravity pulled upon her flesh with unattractive effect. Then she espied what had tickled her—it was the fox tail from the drawer, and it protruded from her arse!

"Lovely, is it not?" Alastair inquired, striding back to her and admiring the tail from behind.

Oh...*my*. Was it truly lovely, an adornment and not a form of degradation? Was being made to resemble an animal provocative or demeaning? A part of her now regretted the exploration of her curiosity. Was this what she was truly willing to submit to? Did this amuse Alastair? Please him? She wanted to please him, but perhaps not at the expense of her dignity.

"This is what you desired, is it not?" he asked. "If you were at Château Follet, you would have to submit yourself to such things—and more."

Her mind whirled as she wondered if Katherine had allowed herself to be locked in the pillory and have a tail affixed to her. Mildred supposed she must have or such articles would not be in her house.

"Oof!" Mildred grunted when Alastair slapped her rump. Her body squeezed the object inside her, and the tail swished against her. Trying to avoid the tickling of its softness, she bent her knees.

Her attention having been focused on her backside, she had barely noted that Alastair had not replaced his fall. But when he positioned himself behind her, she took full notice of his beautiful shaft. He flipped the tail over her rump, and in one swift motion, speared himself into her.

She let fall an unladylike oath. *Ye Gods! Ye Gods!* To be filled in *two* places at once was...marvelous.

She glanced at the looking glass to see that it was truly happening, though she needed no evidence beyond the extraordinary sensations engulfing the whole of her lower half. When he moved inside of her, the sensation called attention to the fullness in her arse, which, in turn, accentuated the fullness in her cunnie. The delectable pressure, assaulting her from all angles, overwhelmed her ability to think. Her legs wanted to buckle beneath the weight of such carnal delirium, but doing so would inflict unwanted tension on her neck and wrists, and Alastair held her up by the hips.

Gradually, he quickened his thrusts. She shot toward her summit with such rapidity that she forgot to ask permission to spend.

But before she could round the peak of euphoria, he stopped.

"M–May I spend?" she recalled. "My lord?"

He withdrew. Her cunnie clutched desperately at emptiness.

"At Château Follet, submissives must earn the privilege of spending," he explained.

Yes, yes, she understood that. Had she not earned the privilege yet?

He sauntered to the front of the pillory and stroked his cock before her. His shaft glistened with her moisture.

"How may I?" She tried to form a coherent sentence. "How may I earn the privilege, my lord?"

He presented his erection to her. Eagerly, she opened her mouth. She would do anything he wished to merit his cock in her cunnie again. To demonstrate her willingness, she licked at the crown of his shaft before swallowing it, tasting the nectar of her own desires upon him.

She sucked until her cheeks caved inward and triumphed at his moan. He bucked his hips at her, and she consumed as much of him as she could. At times she took in too much, and she choked. He popped his cock out to give her a chance to recover before sliding back in. Her cheeks became sore, but her cunnie demanded that she persist. When she became better accustomed, Alastair gripped the pillory and pumped himself more vigorously into her mouth. During their last encounter, he had not spent inside her, but she believed this time he would.

He drove himself deep into her, and she gagged. Only this time he continued to batter her mouth. She tried to pull back to attain some relief, but the pillory prevented it. His cock struck the back of her throat several times, and then her mouth was filled with a hot saltiness. Some of it slid past her lips. Not knowing what he expected, she decided to swallow the rest.

With a roar and much shuddering, he bucked a few more times before retreating.

"Open," he commanded, grabbing himself and aiming his cock at her mouth. More of his seed landed on her tongue. She swallowed and licked her lips.

"My God," he breathed, his legs trembling and his breath shaky. He appeared rather vulnerable, and she felt a heady accomplishment at being able to bring him to such a state. Surely she had earned her privilege now?

But he was not yet done. When he presented his cock to her once more, she gathered she was to cleanse him. She licked and sucked his shaft clean.

Then, to her mortification, he covered himself with his fall and did the buttons.

"Did I not please you, my lord?" she asked.

"You pleased me greatly."

Perhaps he intended to make her spend without his cock, but he set about removing the magnets from her nipples.

"Did I earn the privilege to spend, my lord?"

"Not yet."

Astounded, she said nothing at first. "What more am I to do, my lord?"

"For tonight, nothing."

"Nothing?"

"I will make an assessment tomorrow."

"Tomorrow!"

He popped the tail from her arse.

"Do you tease me or do you mean to be cruel?" she cried.

He gave her a stern look, as if she were being wayward child, but she could not overcome her indignation. Her body was near to bursting. He had had his release. Why was he denying Millie hers?

"I did what you bid," she argued, "without complaint. I permitted you to lock me in this pillory, pin a tail 'pon me arse—"

"You wanted to satisfy your curiosity."

"Yes, but...I thought—we are not finished for the night?"

"We are, and if you wish me to unlock the pillory, you will refrain from further objections."

She nearly objected to his warning but had enough presence of mind to remain silence. He opened the pillory, and she welcomed the opportunity to stand. She did not think she could withstand more time in the device.

Deciding that a question was not a demurral, she inquired, "What were my failings, my lord?"

"You had no failings," he replied.

"Then how is it I did not earn my privilege to spend?"

"You desired an experience equivalent to what might be had at Château Follet. I am granting your request, Millie."

He picked up her shift and robe and presented them to her. She received them unhappily.

"It is customary for the submissive to attend to the keeping and cleaning afterwards," he said, "but I shall see to it for tonight."

She only frowned and hoped that, once in her own bed, she could achieve the climax she had been denied. In a hurry, she slipped on her garments, cursed herself for trusting a self-ish profligate, and turned for the doors.

Alastair grabbed her arm. "You may touch yourself, but you shall not spend, not till I have granted you permission."

"But we are done."

He lowered his voice. "Obey, and I promise you that your reward will exceed all expectation."

His voice made the heat churn inside of her as a shiver went up her spine. Oh, why would he not take her again?

"You will learn the power of anticipation."

"And the agony of denial," she retorted.

He smiled and kissed her brow before releasing her. "Good night, Millie."

This small gesture of affection took her by surprise and thawed a little of her anger. "Good night, my lord."

Deciding that she would only torment herself further by staying in his company, she took her leave. As she walked down the corridor, the moisture between her legs reminding her of her lack of fulfillment, she contemplated that he could hardly know whether or not she had spent. And the tension in her needed release.

But he trusted her. And if he should question her, could she lie to him convincingly? She wanted to obey him, wanted to honestly earn this reward that would *exceed all expectation.* She shivered again and embraced herself, wondering what he could intend.

In the privacy of her bed, sleep eluded her. She tossed and turned, trying not to recall the events of the night, how his touch enthralled her, how his kiss had enflamed her, how his cock had penetrated her.

She rubbed her thighs together in frustration and tried thinking of the less savory moments. However, there was not a moment that she did not, upon reflection, find arous-ing. The discomfort of the pillory, the degradation of the fox tail, somehow had conspired to titillate. The smarting of her arse from the crop, the pinching of the magnets upon her nipples, the gagging from having her mouth stuffed with cock—she would gladly suffer them again.

Giving in, she fit her hands between herself to stroke her clitoris. With a sigh, she fondly recalled how he had pounded into her from behind. Desire renewed itself in her loins. She wanted to spend.

But he had not granted her permission. Had expressly forbid it and promised a greater reward if she complied. She did not doubt that Alastair could deliver upon his word. She wanted that reward.

Reluctantly, she withdrew her hand, rolled onto her stomach, and stuffed her hands beneath the pillows. The night loomed long. She tried to fill her mind with less savory thoughts: how close she had come to marrying Haversham, the number of times he stepped on her toes and Mr. Carleton and his support of slavery,.

Try as she might, she could not ignore the pulsing between her thighs. She drew her hands from beneath the pillows.

CHAPTER THIRTEEN

WHEN MILDRED ENTERED THE BREAKFAST parlor looking a little fatigued, Alastair felt a modicum of guilt at having denied her an orgasm last night, but he reminded himself that it was all for her benefit, and he fully intended to reward her tonight if she succeeded in adhering to his wishes.

Perhaps he ought to have waited until she had become more comfortable with the thought of being penetrated in the arse, but by God, she did look quite the lovely sight with that fox tail dangling between her legs. He thought, too, that he ought not have fucked her mouth with quite so much vigor, nonetheless, his actions were far more gentle than what might be had with another at Château Follet. But he knew it had not all been torment for her last night. Her desire to spend proved it.

Feeling a tug at his groin, he shifted where he sat. Having finished his breakfast, he sat apart from the others with the newspaper and watched as Millie accepted a cup of coffee.

"Did you sleep well, my dear?" Katherine asked. "You appear weary."

Alastair thought he detected a blush in Millie's cheeks, but she kept her gaze lowered. He wondered if she would dare look at him.

"I think I had perhaps too much tea late in the day, and that kept me awake," Millie replied.

"I fear the toast and ham are no longer warm, but I can have fresh toast and eggs brought up."

"That won't be necessary, my lady. I am more than happy with what is here."

After seeing his daughter take but a nibble of the toast, Mr. Abbott said, "You must partake of more, Millie. The bread is freshly baked, and the eggs are but the day-old. You'll not find a finer breakfast."

"But not too much," Mrs. Abbott objected. "A young woman must mind her figure. While a dowry of four thousand pounds may go far, a woman's appearance still is of significant value to the other sex. Though her current form is acceptable, Millie could certainly benefit from losing a little of her weight."

Millie gazed deeper into her cup of coffee.

"I do not think your daughter wants for anything more," said Katherine. "She is lovely as she is."

"That is most generous of you to say, my lady, and we are appreciative of your kindness. A mother wants only what is best for her daughter. Millie benefits from the gowns she wears. The looseness of the skirts hides her form."

As one who had seen her—all of her—without clothing, in bare naked glory, Alastair was a little tempted to respond that Millie's form was more than acceptable. True, it was not perfect, but he had come to appreciate her wider hips and even the roundness of her belly. She was still delightful to the touch.

Sitting at the second table, Thomas asked, "How shall we amuse ourselves today, Papa? May we go hunting?"

"Yes, I think that would be in order," replied Edward. "By all means, let us all have a hunt."

"I think I shall stay inside and read," said Jason.

"What? Not go hunting on such a fine day as this?"

"Would you like to stay and knit purses as well?" Thomas

mocked his brother.

"No, no, my boy. We will all take part in the sport."

It was decided then that the men would go hunting, while the women would prepare a picnic to be shared by all at the end of the hunt. But as the men expected to be hunting for a length, Mrs. Abbott deemed she had enough time to sit and rest a while upon the veranda. Mrs. Cheswith would pen a letter to her sister-in-law while Katherine would finalize preparations for the Michaelmas dinner.

"I will keep you company," Katherine offered to Millie when the others left their tables to prepare for the day's activities.

"I would not keep you, my lady," said Millie as she accepted a second cup of coffee. "I know you must have matters to attend."

"Perhaps Alastair can keep you company for a few minutes."

He halted on his way out of the room, and was prepared to decline his aunt's uninvited suggestion, when Millie responded, rather quickly, "I am perfectly at ease in my own company."

At that moment, Kittredge stumbled into the room. He shielded his eyes from the brightness before taking a seat beside Mildred.

"Good morning, Lady Katherine," he greeted.

"Ah, I have company now," Millie remarked. "There is no need for you to stay."

Katherine rose from her seat, but Alastair decided to remain, curious as to why Millie was so eager to be rid of his company. It was she who had insisted that their interactions remain as they were despite what had transpired between them at Château Follet.

"I will stay with my guest," he offered.

"Ha!" Kittredge grumbled. "Since when do you care to

extend me such courtesies?"

"Is it not enough I make my cellar available to you?"

"I own it is more than enough."

"As I have finished," said Millie, rising from the table, "I will leave you gentlemen in each other's company.

"Sit," Alastair bid. "You will not want Kittredge to think his presence has driven you away."

She looked at him as if to say "indeed, it is your presence that I wish to avoid." Instead, she gave Kittredge a smile before retaking her seat.

"Finish your toast," he said after noticing she had barely eaten half.

"I am no longer hungry."

"You will require sustenance to see you through the activities of the day—and evening."

"A woman must mind her figure."

He lifted his brows at her resistance. "You are fortunate not to be my daughter, or such *disobedience* would merit *punishment*."

She drew in a sharp breath and pressed her lips together. She knew he had chosen his words with purpose. He stared at her, daring her to continue her defiance. She looked at her toast, applied a little more jam, and took a bite.

"What are to be the day's activities?" Kittredge asked between mouthfuls of ham and toast.

"The men are to go hunting," Millie answered, "and we shall all have a picnic afterwards."

"And what of the evening? What is planned?"

Millie looked to Alastair, but he said nothing, waiting to see how she would reply.

"Nothing as of yet," she said. "Lady Katherine's nieces are expected today, and we shall certainly want their opinion if they are not too tired from their travels."

"I had thought from what Alastair said that something had

been decided upon."

A blush crept up her cheeks, but she replied with calm, "I would hazard that Alastair's evening plans entail a hearty round of cards or dice, though I wonder that it will satisfy him, as our play will not rival what he is accustomed to at his gaming hells."

"Not to worry. I take it that is why he brought me along, though I doubt even he would rude enough to expect that the ladies will match his level of play."

"I absolutely would," said Alastair, as Millie replied, "He absolutely would."

They glanced at each other. Kittredge laughed. "By Jove, she knows you well, Alastair. And dares to show it. Your bravery is impressive, Miss Abbott."

"We shall see where her bravery lands her," Alastair said, his hand itching to deliver a spanking. He had the satisfaction of seeing her disconcerted, but his cousin would not be cowed.

"Surely you are not threatened by what you must own to be an honest assessment of your character? Your candor of your faults is what is impressive."

"Ah, you have redeemed yourself, Miss Abbott," Kittredge praised. "I would be hard-pressed to find a compliment for Alastair. You are clever as well, Miss Abbott."

Alastair gazed upon Millie. She spoke with sincerity and, when she was critical of him, there was not the judgment of how he ought to behave. For that reason, he allowed her remarks to pass. "Finish your toast, Miss Abbott."

"Does he always order you about in such fashion?" Kittredge asked.

"Does he not do the same with everyone? He has quite the high opinion of himself."

That was a jibe. Alastair reconsidered the tolerance he granted his cousin. Her spanking would require more than his hand. Perhaps the paddle.

"Oh, he bullies me about all the time, but I welcome it, for he would only do so if he considered it worth his while. Thus, he considers *you* worth his while. It is quite the compliment, for very few satisfy this criterion for him."

"I think you credit me too much, Mr. Kittredge. He only orders me about because it amuses him to vex me."

"Do you think so? Then subvert his goals and pay no heed to what he says."

Alastair grinned at the difficult place Millie found herself in, though Kittredge had intended his advice to be friendly.

"She disobeys at her peril," Alastair drawled. "Finish your toast, Millie."

"Good God, man, are you her father and she a child?"

She frowned, clearly not wanting to capitulate to his orders before Kittredge, but not wanting the consequences of defying her cousin.

"Surely he jests!" Kittredge said. "What can he do to you?"

"I must be careful, Mr. Kittredge," Millie said. "I am afforded a dowry thanks to his generosity. He can give or take it away as he pleases."

"Or raise it," Alastair said.

"You see, I am at his mercy, Mr. Kittredge."

"No, no, Alastair is not as bad as that," his friend protested. "He would not hold your dowry hostage and cares not about your toast. Finish it only if it pleases you."

"Your attempts to play the white knight are unwarranted here," Alastair said. "Miss Abbott is no maiden in need of rescue. She is quite adroit at getting what she wants."

"And now he means to impugn my character," Millie said, putting her hand to her brow in mock despair.

"You, sir, truly are a blackguard," Kittredge declared.

"Stop. I cannot have you at odds. Alastair has few friends, and I will not have your friendship sullied. I will eat the toast to keep the peace." She took a large bite.

Alastair allowed her the escape she had conjured. He was confident she would have eaten the toast to satisfy him.

"There now," she said when she had finished off the toast. "Are you pleased, my lord?"

"Do not test my patience again," he warned.

Kittredge shook his head. "I hope you do not intend to browbeat your future wife in this manner. I wonder that Lady Sophia would endure such behavior."

Millie sat at attention. "Future wife?"

"If this is how treats the fair sex, I doubt any woman would have him."

Alastair said nothing. He had no doubts that he could train Lady Sophia to be as obedient as his dogs, but, for the present, it was more amusing to compel Millie into obedience.

"Alastair will never want for marital prospects."

"I suppose not. Well, Miss Abbott, accept my condolences for your forced kinship to the man."

"Kittredge," Alastair said, "knows full well that if I bid him eat toast, he would do it."

"I would indeed. I am far too invested in his collection of burgundy—I swear he must purchase his wine from smugglers—to risk losing his friendship over a piece of toast. And I suppose Miss Abbott is indebted to you for her dowry, or such an intelligent woman would not heed you in the least."

Alastair did not dispute his friend, but Millie knew full well that he had other forms of persuasion. Breakfast being at an end, Kittredge offered his arm to Millie. Alastair was content to walk behind them. The silly business with the toast had arisen on a whim, but he was satisfied that he had put Millie on notice and even discomfited her a little. He suspected, however, that Millie would not be easily cowed.

He would have to assert himself even more if he were to convince her that she was no match for the Château Follet and its practices.

CHAPTER FOURTEEN

---◇◈◈◈◇---

THEY HAD NOT AGREED TO take their role-playing beyond the night, beyond the doors of the play room, Mildred huffed as she scanned the book titles in Lady Katherine's library. She could only put half her mind, however, to the task of finding a good book for Jason. Her time at breakfast with Alastair and Kittredge still rankled her. If he had made a polite request for her to finish her toast, she might have done so without protest.

No, she would've pointed out that what she ate was no affair of his. She had asked for this, after all, though she had not considered breakfast to be part of the arrangement. Nevertheless, she had invited him to take the role of dominant, and she had been more than willing to submit to his commands last night.

Last night. Her body flushed at the memories. She could hardly wait for tonight. Should she confess that she had been unable to follow his bidding, unable to withhold herself from spending? But then, what might he do? Would she have lost any chance of experiencing the reward he had promised? Could she, perhaps, find a way to make up for her misstep?

She would have time to think on it while Alastair and the rest of the men were out hunting.

She returned to looking at the books on the bookshelf. There were a good many books she thought Jason would enjoy. She wondered if he had read *Gulliver's Travels* by Jonathan Swift? She pulled the book from the shelf.

"I hope you will not make it a habit to disagree with me?"

She whirled around to find Alastair standing inches from her. His nearness ruffled her more than she liked.

"Perhaps I would not if you were not so overbearing," she replied after she had regained her balance. "I was not aware that our arrangement last night allowed you to order me about at all times."

He took a step closer, and she would have retreated if the bookcase behind her did not block her.

"It most certainly did. Perhaps next time you will be more careful with what you request."

She bristled, though he had a point. "And do you approach me now to order me about some more?"

"I do indeed."

Her pulse surged. She glanced past him to see that they were alone.

"I do not think we shall be discovered, but let that be an incentive for you to comply as swiftly as possible."

She embraced the book she held as if it were a shield that could protect her. She looked up at him. "What is it you wish?"

Instead of answering, he closed the distance between them, bumping her into the bookshelf. He curled his fingers about the back of her neck and pressed her chin up with his thumb. She quivered inside as her breath grew uneven. He gazed down at her, and she saw his pupils dilate. Did he mean to kiss her? She very much hoped he would.

When he lowered his head, she closed her eyes so that all her senses could focus on the touch of his lips upon hers. The kiss was soft and gentle but set off a riot inside her body. Desire flamed anew.

With his hand still wrapped about her neck, he pulled her

even closer so that his mouth pressed hard against hers. He parted her lips with his and took mouthfuls of her, sweeping her breath away. The book slid from her grasp, and he grunted when it landed upon his boot.

"Sorry," she mumbled.

He slammed his body into hers, pinning her to the shelves, before resuming his assault upon her mouth.

As much as his kisses thrilled her, she murmured, "Alastair, we must not."

She made a feeble attempt to push him away with a hand, but he pinioned the offending hand to the bookcase. She was trapped. And the possibility that they might be discovered in a compromising way toyed with her ardor.

"Someone might come upon us." She gasped as his mouth trailed to her neck. When his lips caressed her throat, the last of her resistance melted. She wrapped her free arm about him and threaded her fingers through his soft dark locks. She tilted her hips toward him, and she thought she could feel the hardness at his crotch.

He slammed his pelvis into her, making her head whirl. Lust overcame discretion, and she moaned as he kissed whole patches up and down her neck. His hand slid from her neck to cup a breast. She wished she did not have to wear stays so that she could better feel his hand upon her. Nonetheless, she thrilled to his every touch. When he moved his hand to her back, she relished being in his embrace. Truly, there was nothing this man could do that did not excite a response from her body.

Their lips joined once more, and she kissed him back. There was no consideration of what the end would be, for perhaps their actions would only stoke an aggravation that could not be satisfied till later that night. It might even be his intention to set her up for torment, for surely he did not intend to take her here in the library. Yet, knowing this, she could not stay herself from the present temptation. If they were to cease, he would have to initiate it.

He withdrew to give her a chance to catch her breath, and, pressing his forehead to hers, he asked, his own breath a little haggard, "Are you wet?"

"I am not certain. Perhaps."

He took a step back and began unbuttoning his fall. Her eyes widened.

"On your knees, my dear."

"Not *here*. Alastair!"

But his cock sprang free. She could not help but stop and admire the stiff and ready pole, but her senses appealed once more. "This is your aunt's home!"

"Katherine would be the least astonished."

She looked to the door.

"If you are worried, I suggest you act quickly."

She was still flustered but sank to the ground. She clasped her hand about his delightful member. A sound in the corridor made her scramble back up to her feet, but the doors to the library remained closed. She looked to Alastair to see if he had changed his mind, but he only waited. Relenting, she settled herself back on her knees, took his cock in hand, and fitted her mouth over its tip.

Dear God, what had she gotten herself into?

Taking her by the back of her head, he guided her mouth farther down his shaft. She licked and sucked, hoping he would not expect a long session of swallowing cock. He emitted a low groan. She tried to take all of him, but she could not relax enough to do so. He shifted his hand to the back of her neck so that he would not muss her hair and guided her up and down his shaft.

Surely he did not intend to make her suck his cock till he spent? But fearing that he would, she attended to his cock with as much vigor as she could. And perhaps, if she pleasured him to completion, he would not think to inquire as to whether or not she had succeeded in following his orders last night.

Heat swirled in her loins, for she wished such easy attention could be had for her cunnie. She enjoyed his cock, even tasting the saltiness of his seed. Having one's mouth stuffed with cock was so wanton, so depraved. But most of all, though it seemed he battered her with his weapon, it was he who was at her mercy, his desires succumbing to her application. She liked knowing that she could arouse him to such hardness. She could sense his desperation in the way he bucked his hips at her. He was near to spending.

"Let not a drop fall," he warned.

With a muffled roar, he dispensed his seed.

She had nowhere to turn, for he held the base of her head still. The hairs at his groin nearly tickled her nose. A tangy flavor filled her mouth as she tried not to balk at the load. She swallowed as best she could with his cock still in her mouth and gagged a little. His mettle threatened to drip from her mouth, but she swept it back in with her fingers.

He withdrew his cock, allowing her to finish swallowing, before aiming it once more at her mouth. The tip grazed her cheek before entering. She swirled her tongue about his member to lick it clean.

Nothing could surpass the wantonness of what she had just done. And she had done it in Lady Katherine's library. It was more than fortunate that no one had come upon them, but there was no denying that the fear of being caught added to the titillation.

"My God," Alastair breathed before withdrawing for the final time.

When he fixed a starry gaze upon her face, she returned an impish smile.

He went to his knees and, clasping her head in both hands,

crushed his mouth atop hers. The kiss reached into the depths of her mouth, as if he sought to taste himself in her. Heat swirled in her loins, and she knew for certain now that she was wet between the legs.

"I have something for you," he whispered into her ear.

Her pulse quickened. Would he attend her somehow? Her body desperately desired it, but she did not wish to risk them further.

He buttoned his fall first. From inside his coat, he drew out a small box and opened it. Inside, upon the silk cushioning, lay two silver balls, both of which could easily fit in the palm of her hand.

"What are they?"

"Chinese pleasure balls."

He had her sit upon the floor and lift her skirts.

"I think we should —" she hesitated.

"Do not delay, lest you wish to suffer the consequences later tonight."

Reluctantly, she inched her skirts over her bent knees.

"Farther," he commanded.

She bunched the skirts at the tops of her thighs. He spread her knees apart, and the warmth of her body extended to her cheeks at the exposure. He picked up one of the balls between thumb and forefinger and rubbed it against her folds. Pressing deeper, he coated it with her nectar. Closing her eyes, she leaned back and allowed her head to fall against the books. Perhaps she would risk it. At present, he could put anything to her quim, and she would find it pleasurable.

She gasped and sat up when he pushed the ball inside of her. The second ball soon followed. How odd. She had not guessed that this would be their purpose.

He pulled her skirts back over her legs and assisted her to her feet.

"Oh my," she gasped as the balls moved. They even seemed

to quiver, as if the tiniest hammer were striking her most intimate areas.

"The balls have small weights inside them," Alastair explained.

"Ah." She knit her brows till the balls settled in place.

"They will stay till I remove them."

She stared at him in stunned silence.

"Do your best to keep them. You will not want to constantly replace them."

"I am to walk in these?"

"Till I remove them."

He backed away from her to give her room. She took a small step and immediately felt the movement of the balls. Worried that they might fall out, she clenched her cunnie.

"It is not possible," she murmured.

"I gave you the lightest pair I could find."

She tried another step. "No, no, this is too awkward."

If she were walking in private, she might enjoy these delightful balls. But to have them inside her as she went about the day was too much. And what if she should lose one?

"How long am I to have these pleasure balls?"

"As I said, till I have them removed."

"And when will that be?" She looked to the long case clock at the corner of the room. Would he make her wear these for ten minutes? Half an hour? One hour?

"I have not yet decided. Perhaps all day."

"All day!" she cried.

He bent down and picked up her book, handing it back to her before making his way to the doors.

"Alastair!"

"Be grateful, Millie. If we were at Château Follet, I could make you wear a chastity belt of iron or a loincloth made from nettles."

He turned back to the doors and unlocked them.

Her mouth fell open. "They were locked all this time?"

He grinned. "They were."

She would have liked to have thrown *Gulliver's Travels* at him.

"After you, my lady," he said, opening a door.

She trembled with anger but sauntered toward him. She moaned as the balls rolled and bumped each other, sending ripples throughout her nether region. Seeing his look of amusement, she suppressed the urge to glare at him. She would show him instead her poise, and that she was worthy of the experience she had requested of him.

"Thank you, my lord," she said as she swept by him.

"There you are," exclaimed Kittredge. "Mrs. Cheswith asked if I was to join the hunt, and I thought of passing since Alastair and I have been at it for a few days already. She suggested a ride, and I think it a capital idea. Would you care to join us, Miss Abbott?"

"Thank you, but I think I shall spend a quiet morning reading," she answered. The last thing she wanted, with these balls inside of her, was to be bounced about on the back of a horse.

"But we may never see such pleasant weather again till the spring," said Alastair.

She tried not to scowl at him. "I am a poor rider and would slow the party."

"I doubt Mrs. Cheswith will want to ride fast or break into gallop."

Millie frowned at the thought of the balls bouncing madly inside of her if she were to ride at full gallop.

"I think I shall read, then assist with the picnic preparations."

"My aunt and the servants can attend to the picnic," said Alastair. "You should ride, Millie."

He meant it as a command. What a treacherous man her cousin could be!

"Then let it be a short ride."

Kittredge turned to Alastair. "And will you join us?

"I think I shall."

Her heart plummeted. With Alastair along, there would be no relief for her. The faintest regret began to creep into her. Perhaps it had been unwise to submit her request to Alastair. She eyed him, wondering why he was being so vexing. Was this truly how dominants were at Château Follet? She thought of the Viscount Devon. Would he have made her carry Chinese pleasure balls inside her cunnie while horseback riding? Or was such cruelty unique to her cousin?

She believed the latter.

CHAPTER FIFTEEN

———⬦⬦⬦———

THOUGH IT MIGHT NOT HAVE been clear to the others, Alastair could tell when the jostling discomfited her and knew that the blush in her cheeks was not the result of the occasional breeze that blew their way. Nonetheless, Millie bore the riding well and even appeared to bond with Kittredge over their observations of *him*.

"Alastair has more virtues than is credited to him," Millie said. "For example, he is quite equal and fair in his treatment of compliments and criticism directed at him. He pays neither any heed."

"How true," Kittredge acknowledged. "I had never considered that Alastair possessed any virtues."

"Beyond his wine cellar?"

Kittredge laughed. "Yes, yes. Perhaps most of us do not see his virtues because they are dwarfed by his failings."

"We all have failings, Mr. Kittredge."

"And you are kind to grant your cousin an allowance for his."

Accustomed to Kittredge's mockeries, Alastair said nothing. As he watched Millie stumble off her horse despite Kittredge assisting her, he reminded himself that *she* had requested her situation. Soon enough she would deem that the practices of Château Follet were too much for her.

But he had thought the same before, and she had surprised

him. Just as she had surprised him with how well she had taken his cock in the library. He had not intended to spend, but she had gained in skill somehow. Her hot, wet mouth wrapped about his member had been absolutely divine, and he had approached his climax with stunning speed.

"Are you well, Miss Abbott?" Kittredge asked, holding her arm to steady her. "If you will not mind my saying, you appear rather flushed."

"It is merely from the exercise. I am not much accustomed to riding," she had answered.

"The coloring in your cheeks becomes you."

Alastair, having just dismounted, raised his brows, for Kittredge spoke with uncharacteristic sincerity. He observed the two sharing a smile while he handed his horse to the stable hand.

"Come, Millie," Anne beckoned, "let us exchange these riding garments for more fitting attire for the picnic."

From Millie's expression, Alastair gathered her "more fitting" attire differed little from what she currently wore, but she followed Anne into the house. The men had to change as well, and Alastair decided he would give Millie a reprieve from the Chinese pleasure balls. Stopping her before she entered her chambers, he handed her the box that the balls had come in.

"You may remove them," he told her.

Relief flooded her countenance. "Thank you, my lord. They are wrongly named."

"They brought you no pleasure?"

"Can you imagine being bounced about with two balls inside you? They were the worst possible distraction. I could hardly keep my mind off them."

"You seemed to do just fine, but if they did not arouse you, then they failed in their purpose."

The blush in her cheeks deepened, and he had to agree that

the rosiness became her.

"That is precisely the difficulty! I should not be put in such a state when in the company of others."

"Take heart. Perhaps you shall be rewarded for your sufferings."

He took pleasure in considering the many ways he could reward her, provided that she had followed his directive not to spend.

"HOW LONG DO YOU STAY, Alastair? Alastair!" Louisa's voice broke through his reverie. She had arrived with her husband and daughter a few hours ago. Caroline and her husband were also there.

"Kittredge and I depart the morning after Michaelmas," he answered.

"Why such a short stay?"

Alastair was tempted to quip that it was a longer stay than he had intended, but decided to make an attempt to be civil to his sister at his aunt's table. "I had agreed to meet with Mr. Farnsworth regarding a bill he hopes I will support in the House of Lords."

This seemed to perk Millie's interest. She asked, "What is it Mr. Farnsworth proposes?"

He regretted his answer now, for he had no interest to bring about a discussion of a political nature. He returned to cutting the venison on his plate, but answered, "To raise the destruction of stocking frames to a capital felony."

"And punishable by death?" she exclaimed.

He chewed his venison without looking at her, but she would not leave the subject alone.

"That is unnecessarily excessive! Is the punishment of transportation not harsh enough?"

"Alas, it seems not," said Charles, Louisa's husband. "I understand that more of our soldiers are fighting Luddites than are fighting Napoleon on the Iberian Peninsula."

"We cannot afford to war with our own citizens till the threat of Napoleon is eliminated," added Mr. Abbott.

"But surely there is a better solution than executing our own citizens, men who are merely fearing for their livelihoods," Millie persisted.

"*Merely* fearing?" Louisa asked. "I would hesitate to condone the willful destruction of property."

"I do not condone it, but how does the destruction of property merit the taking of a life?"

Clearly not wanting a divisive discussion involving her daughter, Mrs. Abbott interjected, "Lady Katherine, I cannot compliment your chef enough. I have never tasted venison prepared with such rich flavors! You say you have a French chef?"

"I do, but he does wonders with English puddings," Katherine replied.

Alastair could see that Millie was not satisfied with the end of the conversation, but she took her mother's intimation and returned to eating her dinner. Later, Alastair overheard her ask Kittredge what he thought of the Farnsworth proposal.

"Oh, I never have an opinion on political topics," Kittredge returned. "It is an area that will win you many more enemies than friends."

"I thought perhaps it was the Lady Sophia who compels your return to London more than Farnsworth," Louisa voiced.

"Will you never cease to take an interest in my affairs?" Alastair returned. He knew Louisa favored a match between him and the Duke of Wakecastle.

She huffed. "I *am* your sister."

"While that entails you to have opinions of my affairs, I

am under no obligation to heed them."

Her jaw dropped, though she was hardly new to his rudeness.

"I say, Alastair," Edward tried, "I think my dear cousin merely wishes to understand that all is well with you."

"You are too generous, Edward. What you deem a polite interest is little more than prying." He pushed himself away from the table and rose to his feet.

"I do not deserve such criticism!" Louisa objected.

"Perhaps not," Katherine said, "but you should know by now not to tempt the devil."

"Your pardon, my lady," he said to his aunt, "I will excuse myself before I offend further."

Knowing her nephew well, Katherine waved a dismissive hand. An awkward silence fell upon the table while Louisa continued to fume. This was precisely why he had not wished to attend the gathering for Michaelmas, and he decided then and there that he would refuse any invitation for Christmas.

He would depart Edenmoor on the morrow if he could, but first he had to deal with Millie. It was one event he looked forward to during his stay here, and he had much in store for her.

CHAPTER SIXTEEN

---◇◇◇◇---

"I THINK ANDRE DELIGHTS IN ABUSING me!" Louisa lamented after dinner as they gathered for cards in the drawing room.

"That is what comes of being the first and only son. He was far too pampered in his upbringing," Caroline consoled. Then, realizing that Lady Katherine stood near, she added, "I know not what villainy he would have fallen into if not for the influence of our kind aunt."

Their husbands, not knowing whether to fear their wives or Alastair more, remained silent.

The Abbotts, Lady Katherine, and her son formed one table. Mrs. Cheswith opted not to play. The rest of the men formed another table, leaving Millie to play with Alastair's sisters and Emily. Millie had been grateful not to have had many words with Louisa or Caroline. She had felt the former's study upon her since the lady arrived. But now she would be forced to interact with Alastair's sisters.

"Whist," Louisa declared. "I will play nothing else."

She looked to Millie as if daring her to disagree.

"If it pleases you, Mrs. Wilmington," Millie said in friendly way.

"Now then, Miss Abbott, it seems you have many a political opinion?" Louisa asked as Caroline shuffled the cards.

Millie withheld from saying that she had thus far offered

an opinion on one subject only, but replied that she did.

"If I were you, I would not offer them frequently," Louisa continued. "Men may regard you a *bluestocking*, and even a dowry of four thousand pounds may not influence them to think otherwise."

"I should not hold such men in much esteem if they allowed money to sway their true opinions of me, but I am sorry that I spoke when I did. It was perhaps not the best subject for discourse at dinner."

"Indeed. I mean only to provide the advice of a sister. A young woman who is too outspoken risks being deemed a conceit, and you have no wish to challenge my brother on such matters. Surely you do not expect a member of the House of Lords to consider the thoughts of one less practiced in the affairs of the kingdom?"

"I am not equal to his station," Millie conceded, certain that is what Louisa meant, "but I have not given up hope that his lordship is so dismissive of his fellow men that he will hear nothing of what they have to say."

"Oh, but he is!" Caroline cried. She finished dealing the cards.

Louisa narrowed her eyes. "There are not many in this world who would come to Andre's defense. Most would say he is arrogant, dismissive and discourteous. Boorish, even. No one is spared his disdain, not even his family."

"Especially his family," Caroline added.

"Would you not agree with this assessment of my brother, Miss Abbott?"

Alastair sat at the table beside theirs and could undoubtedly hear many a word.

"I am far too indebted to your family to speak ill of anyone," Millie replied. She could not disagree with Louisa without offending her, nor agree with her without offending the Marquess.

"Is Alastair as generous with others in your family as he is with you?"

"I am not aware of all that he does, but he is better equipped to answer your question."

Millie lost many a hand at whist, for, having to attend to Louisa's questioning with carefully crafted responses, she could not concentrate on her play. When they finally called an end to cards, Millie felt as if she had survived several jousting matches. She knew not what Louisa wished she would say. On the matter of the dowry, she told Louisa, "I would his lordship were not so generous. I certainly do not deserve such charity."

Louisa sniffed. "It is almost unseemly and raises many questions."

"I would his lordship could be persuaded to adjust the amount to a more appropriate sum."

That had seemed to appease Louisa a little. She turned to Caroline. "Have you spoken with him?"

"He has even less regard for me," Caroline replied.

After the card tables were put away, the Abbotts and Lady Katherine declared the hour well past their bedtimes. The Wilmingtons and Brewsters also retired, as the day's traveling had fatigued them. Mrs. Cheswith went to look in on her children, for Henry would often experience nightmares. Edward chose a book to read, and Kittredge had settled himself on the sofa and closed his eyes.

Millie, too agitated with the prospect of meeting with Alastair later, had no wish for the solitude of her chambers.

"Do you come to rebuke me for my treatment of my sisters?" Alastair asked when she approached the sideboard where he stood.

"I came to pour myself a glass of port," she answered, "and your relationship with your sisters is none of my affair."

"Would you agree they merit my insolence?"

"Even if they should deserve it on the grandest scale, and I do not mean to say that they do, must you respond with insolence?"

He returned a wry grin. "You suffered them with grace. I heard their every word."

Millie sipped the port she had poured.

"You may speak your mind freely with me, Millie. I am well acquainted with the nature of overbearing."

"I had much rather discuss this bill for the destruction of stocking frames."

"And I do not."

"But what think you of his proposal?"

"I am inclined to support Mr. Farnsworth."

"Death ought to be reserved for the worst of crimes."

"The destruction of property is a severe crime, and you pursue this discussion at your peril."

She hesitated, not knowing what he intended, but she could not resign the topic. "Have you no sympathy for the plight of these men?"

He narrowed his eyes at her.

"I do not say that they should go unpunished for their crimes, but it is out of fear for their livelihoods that they resort to such actions."

"What of the mill owners and the laborers who work the stocking frames? Would you stop industry and the progress of technology?"

"Perhaps the weavers and others of their trade would feel less threatened if they had other resources, such as the ability to combine and negotiate with their employees as a collective."

"Such actions are illegal."

"Then repeal the Combination Acts and permit workers to form such societies. What they seek—wages that will prevail with the rising cost of goods—is not unreasonable. But they are rendered unable to help themselves, and the balance of power lies with the mill owners."

"Now is not the time to encourage Jacobinism."

"Is it wrong to want better wages and better working conditions?"

Alastair leaned in toward her and spoke softly so that no one else would hear. "Is your backside prepared to take the consequences of your colloquy?"

Her cheeks burned and she finished the rest of her port in one gulp. "Forgive me if I did not think you so heartless that you would acquiesce to hanging a man without consideration for the arguments against such judgments."

"Such arguments will undoubtedly be made by the likes of Burdett."

"And the likes of me ought have no opinion of value." Vexed, she turned to pour herself another glass of Madeira.

He stayed her hand. "One glass will do for you."

She opened her mouth to protest, but she had no wish to make a scene over an inconsequential glass of wine. Perhaps it was best she retire to her own chambers.

"I will bid you good night, Alastair," she said, setting down her glass and turning on her heels.

"Midnight," he told her. "And not a minute late."

Her heart palpitated. She dared not look back.

Midnight could not come soon enough.

CHAPTER SEVENTEEN

A LASTAIR WAS WAITING FOR HER when she entered the room. Her body's senses heightened at the mere sight of him. He sat in an armchair, a flogger across his lap, and she was pleased to see he wore his nightshirt beneath his banyan, for she hoped he would disrobe and treat her to the vision of his naked body.

He rose from the chair. "Did you succeed in following orders?"

She lifted her chin to meet his gaze. "Yes, my lord."

He searched her face as if looking for falsehood.

"I wanted to have this reward you spoke of," she added.

"And did you find it an easy task to obey my orders?"

She lowered her eyes. "I did not. You saw that I appeared tired this morning. You may satisfy yourself that you cost me quite a sleepless night."

He smiled. "And you will thank me for it."

She looked at him sharply, but remembered her role. "Yes, my lord, thank you."

"What is it you thank me for?"

Bastard, she thought to herself. "Thank you for forbidding me to spend. Thank you for causing me distress and allowing my body to stew in aggravation. Thank you for the opportunity to earn a reward that will make all of last night's torment worthwhile."

"Well said. You may disrobe."

She started. Already? But she was eager to receive the reward, so she untied her robe and cast it aside. She slid off her shift and stood in the buff before him. He circled her, and she tried not to think of the parts of her that might have merited criticism.

"On the table," he said, gesturing to the plain wooden furniture.

She sauntered over and sat down on the surface.

"Lie down."

She did as he bid, allowing the lower half of her legs to dangle over the edge.

"Did you touch yourself while you lay in bed last night?"

"Yes, my lord."

"Show me precisely what you did."

Though it was not the first time she had touched herself before him, she still hesitated, still finding it an embarrassing demand. Nevertheless, she inched her right hand to her mound and caressed the folds below.

"Do you ever fondle your own breasts?"

"At times."

"Why not more often? They are such beauties."

He took her left hand and placed it upon her left breast. "Fondle your tit."

She groped and kneaded herself, hardly believing she was splayed across the top of the table, arousing herself in such wanton display. Despite the embarrassment, her middle finger slid along her clitoris, coaxing hunger between her legs.

"Did you come near to spending on your own?"

"Yes."

"How many times?"

"Some four or five times."

"And you had the fortitude to refrain?"

"...yes."

He attended to her other breast, gripping it, squeezing it, and rolling it over her chest. He pinched the nipple and pulled it lightly.

"Do you wish to try another new item?"

"Yes, my lord."

He went to open the drawer of the sideboard and returned with two small glass tubes. He placed the open end of one over a nipple and pulled the top of the syringe till the cylinder fixed tightly to her, producing a constant tugging of her nipple. He did the same to the other breast. She watched as her rosy buds darkened in color.

He went to stand at the other end of the table and, taking up her leg, placed her feet near her buttocks. As a result, he had a better view her quim.

"Continue your caresses."

She had stalled while marveling at the glass tubes protruding over her nipples. She resumed playing with her clitoris. His thumb joined her, bumping into her fingers as he grazed her flesh.

She moaned as he dipped his thumb toward her slit and caressed the edge of it. She hoped he would enter her. Her cunnie craved to be filled. He rubbed the outside of her slit before sliding two digits into her wet heat. She gasped when he struck a particularly sensitive part inside of her. He knew it, and brushed it over and over. She shivered and writhed, unsure if she could withstand the acute pleasure, yet wanting the torment. But he withdrew and wiped her moisture on her clitoris. Her cunnie yearned for his fingers' return, but she was grateful she could address the tension by caressing her clitoris, which she did at a more ferocious pace.

"Good. I want you to demonstrate how you made yourself spend last night."

She could feel the wave of rapture looming near. "Yes, my lord."

"Then you did make yourself spend."

Her eyes widened. Too late, her fib had been discovered.

He made a tsking sound. "Millie, I am disappointed. And now I will have to punish you for three offenses."

"Three?!"

"Spending without permission, lying, and pursuing a discussion of stocking frames against my advisement."

Her heart sank.

"On your feet," he directed.

Apprehensive but not willing to offend him further, she hopped off and stood before him. He turned her around so that she faced the table.

"Bend over."

"My lord, must our *arrangement* extended beyond these doors?"

"You were warned that there would be consequences."

"I am to obey you at all times—in front of others?"

"Yes." He pushed her down over the table. "What is your safety word, Millie?"

"Pearls."

"There is a good chance you will require its use tonight."

Her breath caught in her throat.

He palmed a buttock. She closed her eyes, relishing his touch. She craned her head and saw him bend down to the ground. A rope circled her right ankle, which was pulled and secured to a leg of the table. The same was done with her left ankle. With her legs spread, he had easy access to her quim. He grabbed her wrists next and bound them behind her back. Unable to prop herself up, her breasts dug into the hard wooden surface. He went back to caressing her rump. She suppressed a purr, lest her display of pleasure should cause him to desist. His hand reached between her thighs and lightly grazed her folds, teasing her. He did this till she was breathless, craving him to touch her harder.

He passed his hand over the arch of her derrière once more, warming her with his touch. "I will deal you twenty-five lashes, and you will thank me after each one."

"Yes, my lord."

She heard him step back and braced herself. The flogger landed on one cheek with mild impact. It almost soothed.

"Thank you, my lord."

The second was similar, but she knew he would graduate to harsher blows.

"Thank you, my lord."

He whipped the falls across her arse with more force. She yelped, but thanked him with ease. The fourth blow landed with the tips of the flogger and stung more. Still, she tolerated the flogging well—till the tenth wallop landed across both cheeks.

The eleventh knocked the breath from her.

"Miss Abbott?"

"Thank you," she said when she had recovered her breath.

"Thank you...what?"

"My lord," she quickly added.

"Too late. You've earned yourself five more."

She made sure to thank him properly on the following whacks. Her arse felt on fire, but the smarting fueled a different heat in her belly, as did the discomfort of having her breasts pressed into the table.

Only when he exchanged the flogger for the cane did she worry. The first blow sent her hips biting painfully into the wooden table. She wailed on the second one, and had to clench her teeth together on the third, but still a cry escaped her.

"This won't do," he remarked. "You'll wake the guests."

He went to the sideboard and searched a drawer till he found an object familiar to her: a collar with a round wooden ball in the middle. He set the ball into her mouth. This one was larger than the one she had taken at Château Follet, and barely fit into her orifice. He secured the collar behind her head. She wondered if he still expected her to thank him.

"Miss Abbott?" he asked after he had dealt a blow that would have knocked her over the table if she had not been bound to it.

"Hunh huh, heh hoh," was her best effort to say "thank you, my lord."

She had lost count and thought perhaps only two more blows remained—no, seven. She had forgotten he had added five more. She blinked back tears after the cane bit into her once more. The wooden ball did not muffle all her cries, and her mouth ached from being stretched. She wondered if she would survive till the end of the punishment.

As if sensing her doubts, he took a respite from the caning and caressed her between the thighs. Relief added to the exquisiteness of his touch. His fingers plied her clitoris, and her body surprised her with how quickly it ascended the summit of pleasure. The burning and aching of her buttocks could not diminish the rapture being stoked beneath.

How was it he knew precisely how to touch her? Would her body always react so favorably to him? The wetness from the earlier attention now flowed down her inner thighs. But surely he would not grant her permission to spend? Or would he have mercy upon her? It seemed the latter, for he continued to stroke her, persuading her body to the edge. She suspected she would not be so fortunate.

Indeed, just as she neared a call, he withdrew, leaving her body in bereft confusion. The cane came down hard on her backside, and she promised that she would never again disobey a direct order of his.

She shrieked at the next unrelenting fall of the cane.

"Do you require your safety word?" he asked.

She took several breaths but eventually shook her head.

She had fallen off a horse once and landed on her arse, but that pain did not compare to what engulfed her rear at present. After he had dealt the final blow, she wondered that she would be able to sit tomorrow.

Setting aside the cane, he rubbed her cheeks, and gently spanked them with his hands. She moaned, not knowing what was worse — the bruising of her derrière or the hollow in her cunnie. It pulsed and clenched in search of attention. She lay with her eyes closed and tried to pretend that she possessed fewer nerves than she did.

She heard a rustling sound behind her, the removing of his clothes, perhaps, and then—a joyous sensation. It was his cock sliding along her folds. Her body came to life, yearning for him to enter her.

He grabbed her hips and, without ceremony, plunged himself in, burying himself to the hilt. It mattered not that he took her so swiftly. She gloried in being stuffed with his cock. The angle of his entry was glorious, touching her in delightful places. She heard him groan before he began pummeling her with his member. His pelvis slapped into her sensitive rump. She grunted with every thrust. Her body, whipped and abused, still exalted in the bliss of their congress, relishing the way his cock battered her. The smarting in her buttocks, the pain of being ground into the wooden table, gave way to the rapture blossoming in her nether regions.

For a fleeting second, she worried that he would spend inside of her, but another part of her cared nothing for caution and wanted only that their bodies reach their natural conclusions.

Alastair withdrew and untied the ropes at her ankles. He turned her around so that she lay on her back and lifted her legs so that her backside was fully upon the table. The lust in his countenance set her ardor soaring. She was glad to be off her breasts, though having her arms pinioned beneath her was no more comfortable.

She watched him walk to the sideboard and return with the tiny magnetic spheres. He clapped them to one nipple. She thought he would do the same to the other nipple but instead he applied them to her folds, pinning them to her clitoris before sinking his cock back inside her.

He threw a leg over each shoulder. The position allowed him to penetrate her deeper. She whimpered at the force of his motions. The little magnetic spheres pinched into her flesh and she longed for more direct stimulation upon her clitoris, but it was clear to her now that she would not receive his permission to spend. He was using her body for his pleasure. His grunting and groaning intensified, and she could not keep up with his pummeling. He jerked out of her and sprayed his hot, sticky mettle over her belly and bosom. A small drop landed on her lips.

She gazed up at the ceiling and watched the shadows flicker. Her mind and body were in a state of disarray.

After he had milked the last of his seed from his cock, he loosened the collar that held the ball and pulled it down past her chin. "Have you learned your lesson, Millie?"

CHAPTER EIGHTEEN

---◇◇◇◇---

HER BODY, MARKED BY HIS seed, was a beautiful sight. He had not wanted to punish her harshly, but she had left him little choice. She had told him a falsehood, and that was unacceptable.

"I learned my lesson, my lord."

"Had we been at Château Follet, your punishment might have been far worse."

After removing the magnets at her nipple and her folds below, he found linen and wiped his mettle from her body before pulling her upright. She winced when her weight came to rest upon her arse.

The sensation of thrusting himself into her—especially as she lay face down upon the table, her full and fleshly arse rounding the edge—had not yet left him. After a few minutes, he could have gone at her again. He wanted to see her spend, wanted her to achieve that carnal glory through him. But he resisted. She needed to learn her lesson in full, without question.

"Are we done, my lord?" she asked.

"For tonight."

He tried to ignore her disappointment and attended to unbinding her wrists. He rubbed them after removing the rope.

"Did I disappoint you, my lord?"

"You endured your punishment well and have atoned for your misbehavior."

"I could have tolerated more."

He spared her a brief glance to see that she was in earnest, then resumed massaging her arms to encourage the circulation to return to the limbs. He did not doubt but that she could have performed well at Château Follet, but his aim was to discourage her, not encourage her. Perhaps he had not been harsh enough, but she had promised him that she would not return to the Château.

"May I have another chance to earn a reward?"

He undid the collar with the ball and wiped it with his handkerchief before replacing it to the sideboard. Picking up a vial of lotion, he returned to where she now stood beside the table.

"Bend over."

"Again?"

"Your position is not to ask but to obey."

"Forgive me, my lord."

She braced herself against the table. Her rump rounded nicely for him. He admired the crimson coloring and the streaks were the cane had landed. Grabbing a buttock, he rubbed it to encourage the flow of blood there in the hopes that it would ease the bruising. He did the same with the other cheek before applying the contents of the vial.

He felt the heat percolating anew as he wondered if he would ever take her in the arse.

"You did not answer my prior query, my lord," she said after he had finished attending to her derrière and stood her up.

"You always have the chance to earn a reward," he answered, handing over her garments. "But I shall require your best behavior for the whole of tomorrow."

"I will not fail this time, my lord."

"There will be no questioning of my directives and no talk of stocking frames."

"Yes, my lord. And I shall refrain from spending or pleasuring myself tonight."

"Succeed, and you shall have your chance to spend, and spend marvelously."

His voice had grown husky of its own accord. Standing less than two feet from her, he was tempted to take her into his arms and kiss her. The sparkle in her eyes, the anticipation in her countenance, caused feelings to swell in his bosom. But he stayed himself.

Instead, he cupped her chin and brushed his thumb over her bottom lip. She was not the woman he had thought her to be upon first meeting her. He had found her polite and intelligent but also plain and uninteresting. Her initial timidity had waned surprisingly quickly, and thereafter she had adopted a nonchalance toward him that he found more acceptable than the receptions he more commonly received from others.

"Thank you, my lord."

The simple words undid his resistance, and he lowered his head to sweep his lips over hers. His arm circled her waist, and he crushed her still naked body to his. He could feel his hardness reviving as his senses took in the scent of her arousal, the sound of her breaths, and the pressure of her lips and body. He could take her again, wanted to take her again, but he would be a poor dominant if he could not retain the discipline he required from her.

Letting her go, he stepped away before desire overcame him. He reached for his own nightclothes.

"I will see to the room," he said after pulling his shirt overhead.

Still in a state of discompose, she took longer to dress. Her backside grazed the table's edge as she bent to pick up the robe she had dropped.

"I think I shall want to stand all day tomorrow," she remarked.

He did not regret the soreness that would plague her the following day. It would be a constant reminder of him, his expectations, and all that had transpired this evening.

"Good night, Millie."

"Good night, Al—my lord."

He would have allowed her the use of his name, and almost wished she had spoken it. After she had left, he sank into the armchair and shook his head.

He would be glad to leave two mornings hence. Millie was having more of an effect upon him than he wanted. Tomorrow evening would be their last. If she failed in her efforts to earn his approbation, he would administer a punishment she would never forget. If she succeeded, he would give her the greatest ecstasy his abilities could proffer.

Either way, he hoped, would end her ever considering Château Follet again. And then he would truly be done with his cousin once and for all.

CHAPTER NINETEEN

─◈◈◈─

THE FOLLOWING MORNING, ALASTAIR WENT fishing with Edward, Thomas and Henry. Thus, he was not present to see Millie after she had come down for breakfast. He imagined her discomfort as she tried to sit to dine, and would take pleasure in inspecting the state of her arse.

The women were all having tea in the parlor when they returned. Henry went immediately to his grandmother to tell how he caught the largest fish of anyone, and Thomas was quick to point out that the fish would have gotten away if not for him. Mr. Abbott dozed in a chair beside the fireplace. Wilmington read the paper while Brewster penned a letter at the writing table. Kittredge sat beside Millie as she and Jason appeared to be discussing *Gulliver's Travels*.

"I am glad to hear that Farnsworth is proposing a bill to discourage the destruction of textile machines," said Wilmington. "This paper says that more of our military have been deployed to Lancashire following an attack on Burton's Mill. The Luddites there have threatened the local magistrates with death if they attempt to interfere. Something must be done. Your meeting with Farnsworth is timely and commendable."

Alastair scanned the room. His niece, Emily, occupied the settee nearest Millie. When Emily met his gaze, she blushed and quickly looked down at her embroidery. She had been casting glances at him since her arrival. He would not normally sit for tea, but he wanted to see how Millie would do in his company. He decided he would take his tea standing.

Millie had looked up when Wilmington spoke, and it seemed she had contemplated speaking, but when she saw Alastair, she remained mute.

"Are you well acquainted with Farnsworth?" Wilmington asked.

"I am not," Alastair replied. "Millie, I will have a cup of tea, if you please."

A few heads turned her way, for she was not sitting nearest to the tea table, but she rose and dutifully poured him a cup.

"But he asked you to meet with him on this important matter?"

"I have little interest in the subject, or in Farnsworth, and agreed to meet with him only because he once granted a favor to my father. I have very little to do with Parliament."

Millie approached with his tea. "Alas, it is a duty you cannot eschew."

"Why not?"

She seemed taken aback. "Because you sit in the House of Lords."

"Not by choice."

"It is both a responsibility and a privilege of the peerage."

"I hardly deem it a privilege. You would not either if you had to sit through a session of Parliament."

"I have read the speeches given by various members. It is a privilege no matter how tedious the task. Your decisions have repercussions on all the citizens—and even creatures—of the crown."

"There are other men who delight in such responsibilities. I am not one of them."

She furrowed her brow. "Have you no sense of *noblesse oblige*, my lord?"

He gave her a stern look. Did she not wish to earn her reward tonight?

"Millie!" Mrs. Abbott exclaimed, bewildered that her daughter dared to speak to him in such a manner. "Lord Alastair, you pardon. Millie, whatever are you on about?"

"Ha! Alastair? *Noblesse oblige?*" cried Louisa. "Clearly you know him little, Millie."

"Louisa is right," he said to Millie. "The care of the citizens is best left to others more capable than I."

But Millie was not prepared to relent, and he found the depth with which she stared at him to be unsettling.

"You delight in being seen as heartless," she said, "but I think we would be gravely mistaken to despair of you so easily."

He returned her stare. "You pay too much heed to my aunt and her opinions of me. She is prejudiced in my favor."

"And do you suggest that her hand in your upbringing was a failure?"

Someone in the room gasped. His jaw tightened but he managed to say, "Thank you for the tea, Millie. You may sit down."

She blinked several times, unaccustomed to taking such direct commands.

"Millie, come!" her mother bade.

She did as told and went to sit beside her mother and Mrs. Cheswith, but she did not appear pacified.

"Millie is right to question you, Andre," Katherine said after setting Henry off her lap. "It would seem you have no regard for my influence in your life."

"If not for you, m'lady, I would be an even worse scoundrel."

"Scoundrel or not," said Wilmington, "it is right of you to meet with Farnsworth and support his proposal. An act of Parliament is required to repress machine-breaking and other violent acts against commerce."

Alastair waited to see if Millie would speak, and she seemed to contemplate it.

"These rebels are as terrible as the colonists in America," offered Caroline. "Who knows what other atrocities they, if unchecked, will commit?"

Millie could not resist. "Perhaps they would not resort to desperate measures if they could find the means to support themselves and their families."

He could hardly believe his ears. Last night, she had sounded so eager to earn his approval. Had she forgotten that he had forbid further talk of this very subject? "By desperate measures, you mean the destruction of *stocking frames*?"

"Yes. If Parliament could see fit to repeal the Combination Acts or consider setting minimum wages, these workers would have more hope."

He stared at her. There was both defiance and fear in her countenance. She had not forgotten. She had simply chosen to disregard him.

"It is not for Parliament to interfere with the economy's natural order," Wilmington responded.

"Workers are part of the economy as well, but our laws prevent them from seeking the most basic necessities. Costs have risen, but wages have not. These workers—and, yes, the Luddites among them—are being denied an ability to seek what every Englishman has a right to: life, liberty and the pursuit of happiness."

Seeing that everyone was staring at her, she withdrew and said nothing more.

"Where does it say every man has such a right?" Wilmington asked.

"My dear Millie, you have an eloquence to your speech," Katherine voiced, "and it is clear you have much charity in your heart. It is easy for our society to overlook the toils and sufferings of the lower classes."

"She has always had much compassion for the poor," Mrs. Abbott said gratefully.

Louisa shared a smirk with Caroline. No doubt they thought that Millie held such an affinity for the less well-off because her family was among them.

Millie avoided his gaze the rest of the time. Kittredge, who had witnessed the scene in silent amusement, approached him to inquire how the fishing went. Louisa persuaded Emily to play her best sonata on the pianoforte. Afforded some of the finest instructors, Emily played extremely well.

"Do you play, Miss Abbott?" Louisa asked when Emily had finished both a sonata and a prelude.

"Not well," Millie replied. "We would benefit from having Miss Wilmington play another piece."

"As well as Emily plays, she is happy to share the instrument. Though her instructor says he has no student who can accomplish a piece as well, and in so short a time as Emily, she is no glutton for attention. I bid you play a little, Miss Abbott."

"Do play, Miss Abbott," Alastair seconded when it was clear that Millie had rather not.

Millie glanced at him. After her earlier defiance, he did not expect that she would disobey him again. She went to the pianoforte and chose to play one of Mozart's simpler sonatinas. Her fingers had not the agility of Emily's, but she performed more than adequately.

"I think I shall collect some of the Michaelmas daisies for our dinner table tonight," said Anne.

"May I join you?" Millie quickly asked.

"Mr. Kittredge, you have not seen the gardens," said Katherine. "Perhaps you would care to assist the ladies?"

Kittredge bowed. "Certainly, my lady."

Caroline, Emily and Mrs. Abbott decided to join Anne

and Millie. Edward decided to take his boys out for a walk with the hounds, to be joined by Wilmington and Brewster. Louisa said she would rest a while in her room. Mr. Abbott continued to slumber beside the hearth.

"You could be kinder to Millie," Katherine told him as they took their leave after all the others.

"Gifting her a dowry of four thousand pounds is not kind enough?" he returned.

"She would rather not have such a gift."

"Am I to blame if she chooses not to appreciate it?"

"Is that why you seem cross with her?"

He nearly replied that it was because Millie had disobeyed her dominant. Katherine would understand then. But, lest Millie had already confessed their nightly activities, he would not reveal them.

"She may not have the finest manners," Katherine continued as they walked down the corridor, "but she means no disrespect."

"Madam, perhaps you had not heard all that she had said, but she dared upbraid me for my lack of *noblesse oblige* before mine own family."

And against my orders, he added silently.

"And that perturbs you, Andre?"

He said nothing at first, for he cared very little what others might say or think of his actions, but her words had rankled him. Feeling his aunt's keen study upon him, he asked, "And you feel I deserve just such a scolding?"

"I do."

"I receive enough from my sisters and you. Louisa, in particular, is fortunate I do not throw her out of my house."

"And do you pay us any heed?"

"No, and you would now add Millie to your party. As a result of our encounter at Château Follet, she now thinks herself entitled to speak to me as she does."

"She was never terribly afraid of you, and I think she will continue so, despite your best efforts to intimidate her."

Ready to end the conversation, he said, "I know you have a fondness for Millie, but I would take care what thoughts and actions you encourage in her."

"You promised, for my birthday, to look after someone."

"And I have done so, but once Millie is married, my responsibility ends."

"No wonder you gave her such a grand dowry."

"Precisely."

He bowed and took his leave. He had to consider what he would do with Millie tonight.

CHAPTER TWENTY

---◈◈◈---

"IN FRONT OF HER LADYSHIP, our host!" Mrs. Abbott cried for the third time as Mildred dressed for dinner in her chambers. Her mother had already reproached her after the tea, and again when they had finished collecting flowers. "Have you gone mad, Millie? Truly, I think there was not one who was not in horror at your behavior."

Mildred hung her head. She regretted challenging Alastair before his family and had no excuse for her lack of manners. The morning had come with promise, for she had succeeded in not spending the night before, but she had ruined her prospects for a reward. His displeasure at her defiance had been obvious.

"I cannot fathom why you would assume such familiarity with the Marquess?" Mrs. Abbott wrung her hands. "I fear for your dowry and should not be surprised at all if he retracted the endowment. Oh, Millie, what were you thinking? How will you atone for what you did? You will have to ask his forgiveness. How I hope he shall forgive you! We must not lose the dowry."

But not everyone had been horrified by her display during tea. During the walk in the garden following, Kittredge had approached her. "Miss Abbott, I must say I am in some admiration at your courage to speak with such frankness to Alastair."

"It is not courage but foolhardiness," she had replied.

"Nonetheless, there are few who would have dared question him as you did."

"I regard the subject with some passion, but I should not have allowed my sentiments to overrule common courtesy."

Before the dinner, Mildred had apologized to Lady Katherine, but her ladyship had dismissed her apology. "Goodness knows Alastair could use a little scolding."

That Lady Katherine had taken no offense did little to cheer Mildred. When she saw Alastair enter the anteroom, her breath caught. But she could not pass the dinner without speaking to him beforehand. Collecting herself, she went to where he stood, conscious that many in the room were gazing upon her.

"My lord, I must ask your forgiveness for my earlier rudeness," she began. "I ought not have spoken in the manner that I did, and my wrong is worse for having done so before your family."

She would apologize for another reason as well, but she could not speak it before company. She hoped that her eyes conveyed what she could not say.

"I accept your apology, Miss Abbott," he said after staring down at her for far too long than was comfortable for her. "I hope that you consider the discussion of stocking frames at an end?"

She hesitated but replied in the affirmative. She curtsied and returned to the other side of the room. Though he had sounded sincere in forgiving her, she thought she had best not put herself in his way.

A footman entered to announce that dinner was ready. Alastair presented his arm to his aunt, but Lady Katherine had hooked her arm through Thomas's.

"It is not often I have the pleasure of having my grandson escort me to dinner," her ladyship declared.

There was a brief moment of awkwardness as the others wondered how to proceed, as Lady Katherine had upended the proper order.

Alastair, unruffled, turned to Mildred. "Miss Abbott."

Surprised, she could only stare at his proffered arm. Louisa's eyes widened. Mildred was tempted to protest that he ought to escort Miss Wilmington, who had more standing, to dinner but that would only call further attention to the situation. She accepted Alastair's arm, and Kittredge was left to escort Miss Wilmington.

Fortunately she did not have to sit near Alastair during the dinner and was near enough to Kittredge that she could hear his easy, affable talk of the theater and how Charles Kemble was to perform in a production of *Hamlet*. But Mildred could enjoy little else of the goose, baked turnips and pie. After dinner, she declined to join the rest in cards and chose to read in the corner of the drawing room, but the words blurred often. She wanted to ask Alastair's and Lady Katherine's pardons once more, though she knew the former would abhor the necessity of exchanging more words and the latter would deem it unnecessary.

"Papa, I have been the rudest of guests," she said when her father had approached. The card tables were put away, and Miss Worthington was to play the pianoforte again.

"Your mother told me what had transpired. As it cannot be undone, all that you can hope to do is ask their pardon, which you have done."

"I must ask your pardon as well, for my want of manners must reflect poorly on our family."

"You could not do worse than your Uncle Stephen."

Her mother's younger brother had run off with a married woman, but this offered little consolation to Mildred.

"I doubt Lady Katherine was much troubled by it."

"Even if she were, she is too kind to speak of it."

"Are you certain? She strikes me as a woman who is most comfortable with speaking her mind."

Mildred had to agree that she saw and heard little from her ladyship that indicated she thought less of Mildred for what had happened. Nevertheless, she would not permit herself any leeway. "But I criticized her nephew before her family!"

"As for the Marquess, I doubt he heeds what anyone says of or to him. You could call him a blackguard or worse, and I doubt he would be disturbed in the least."

"I think I would like a cordial," Mildred started before her father could complete his sentence, for Alastair stood behind him

Mr. Abbott, seeing her widened eyes, turned about, colored, and stuttered, "Cordial, yes—yes, you, er, wished for a glass of—of cordial?"

With a curt bow to Alastair, Mr. Abbott hurried away. Mildred felt her heart sink. How many more times would her family offend Alastair? She found solace in the fact that the Marquess was to depart on the morrow.

"You may find page ninety-one instructional for your situation," Alastair said, handing her a book before walking away.

She turned to the page he'd named and saw a note:

Midnight.
Your punishment awaits.

Her punishment. She both welcomed and dreaded it. But she would suffer whatever punishment he would mete out. Closing the book, she looked at the clock. It was just past nine o'clock. She would pass the next few hours in anxious anticipation.

CHAPTER TWENTY-ONE

A VIBRANT FIRE GREETED HER AS she entered the chambers at the appointed hour. Alastair, in his nightshirt and banyan, stood with his arms crossed before him. Without forethought, she knelt at his feet.

"Forgive me, my lord."

"I accepted your apology already, Millie," he said.

"That was for speaking before your family. I now ask your pardon for having defied your wishes."

"You will atone for that tonight. And I had thought you intended to earn a reward."

"I did have such intentions. But…I should have waited to voice my opinions to you in private."

"Then you do not regret what you said? Only that it was said in company?"

She kept her gaze lowered. "My thoughts on the topic have not changed, my lord, and needed to be voiced."

"Then why ask my pardon now?" He sounded slightly baffled.

"Because I had not wanted to disappoint you. In hindsight, I should not have agreed to a command I could not follow. When you were so dismissive of your duties—well, I will take what punishment you intend, my lord. May I suck your cock for you, my lord?"

He threaded his hand in her hair and yanked her head back

so that she could meet his gaze. "You will beg for cock soon enough, my girl, but you will have it only upon completion of your punishment."

"Yes, my lord."

He released her. "Show me your arse."

She bent over and pulled her robe and gown up to her waist. He palmed a cheek. She tingled beneath his touch.

"There is barely any bruising," he noted. "It can take more abuse tonight."

"Yes, my lord. I hope you will spank me well."

He grunted. "On your feet."

She rose from the floor and stood at attention.

"Remove the robe," he said.

When she had slid out of the garment, he stood behind her, close enough to make her every nerve come to life. "I take it you did not bring yourself to spend last night?"

"I did not, my lord."

Reaching an arm around her, he cupped a breast through her shift. "Was it difficult to obey my orders in this?"

She let out a haggard sigh. "Yes, my lord."

"Did you touch yourself?"

"I dared not, as doing so had led to my failure my first night."

He rolled the orb against her chest as he hardened and released his grip. "How did you refrain? How did you relieve the agitation?"

"I pressed my legs together."

"You were very wet between the legs last night."

She gasped when he pinched her nipple through her shift. "I paced the room for a while. Then, I was wearied enough to fall asleep."

"And how was your arse when you woke this morning?"

"Sore."

"Did you enjoy being in such a state?"

"Yes, my lord."

He pulled her shift down one shoulder and kneaded the exposed breast. He pulled her into him. "Your body will want to spend desperately tonight."

She moaned at the thought, relishing the hardness of his body at her back.

"Do you deserve to spend?" he asked, his other arm snaking around her hip to clasp her mound.

"No, my lord."

He rubbed her between the thighs. It did not take long for the wetness to begin. Feeling his cock harden behind her, she wanted her body to meld with his, for the hand at her beast to become a permanent part of her. But she should forebear the rising warmth in her. He would only leave her bereft. She braced herself against his delectable fondling.

"You will want your arousal," he advised, "to survive your punishment."

In truth, she could not resist his ministrations. They felt far too divine. The man could arouse her at any time, in any place. He had only to speak to ignite the heat inside of her.

The fabric he rubbed into her folds, though damp now, created a pleasurable friction. He lightly pinched her nipple before moving his hand to her throat. Her head fell back to his chest as the rest of her writhed against him. She panted and slipped further into the pool of desire.

But as she expected, he eventually withdrew, leaving her bereft. He went to the sideboard and returned with the ball and collar.

"We will need to quiet your cries," he explained.

"But how will I speak the word 'pearls,' my lord?"

"You did not question it last night."

"I expect the punishment tonight will be worse."

"And it will be."

She studied his face. How vexed was he at her?

"I will give you the choice, but be aware that your screams may be heard."

"I will take the collar, my lord."

He affixed the implement about her head, then pulled from the pocket of his banyan his neckcloth, which he wrapped over her nose and mouth. "This should sufficiently muffle your cries."

Her heart hammered, and it would have been difficult to swallow, even absent the ball stretching her mouth. She did not like the linen as her breaths felt warm and stifled.

He stood two feet from the wooden table. "Approach."

She went to him. He turned her to face the table, then pulled the rest of her shift down. She ought to be accustomed to standing naked before him, but still an uncomfortable awareness filled her.

"Reach for the table."

She bent over and braced her arms against the table's edge. She was bent nearly in half at the waist, her breasts dangling beneath her. He walked over to the wall before returning to stand behind her.

She gave a small shriek before falling into giggles as feathers brushed her derrière, but it was not easy to laugh with the ball stuffed in her mouth. She closed her eyes as she tried not to heed the tickling. Thankfully, it did not last too long.

Her next shriek was altogether different as a wooden paddle collided with her backside. She lost her grasp against the table and stumbled.

"Resume your position, Miss Abbott."

Her mind whirled, wondering how many of these blows she could endure, but she braced herself against the table once more. He pulled her a step farther so that her rump rounded more fully for him.

Smack!

Inadvertently, she bit into the ball. Now her teeth hurt.

The third blow made her knees buckle. He waited till she righted herself before delivering the fourth whack. Tears pressed against the back of her eyes, and her saliva began to seep from between her lips and the ball. He waited for the full effect of the sting to dissipate before swinging the paddle to her rump again. She gave a sob and thought of her safety word, but she would not have wanted to use it. She wanted to endure the punishment. Having failed him before, she did not want to do so again.

But by the tenth blow, she would gladly have parted with her arse forever. Her arms shook, and the tears in her eyes had spilled. The feathers returned, stoking the stinging to new life. The linen wrapped about her had become suffocating. She told herself that she deserved this punishment, but a part of her questioned this premise. She had been forward with him; it was not her place to comment on how he handled affairs of Parliament. But, in truth, his disposition merited comment. She reminded herself that she ought not have spoken so in front of his family. This surely deserved a sound punishment, but she hoped he was done with the paddling. Even if she wanted to, she doubted that she could endure much more.

With immense relief, she saw him return the paddle to where it had hung upon the wall. He came back with a long cord of rope. Reaching beneath her, he wrapped the rope around one breast, crossed it to the other, did the same, and crossed it back before securing the end of the rope. The bindings formed a vise about her orbs, squeezing and misshaping them.

"You may stand, Millie."

She did as told, brushing away the tears so that he would not see them. He stood before her and looked deep into her eyes.

"You did well, Millie. Now we may commence with the second part of your punishment."

CHAPTER TWENTY-TWO

---◇◆◇◆◇---

S HE HAD WIPED AWAY THE tears, but he still saw some swimming in her eyes. The paddling had hurt. Though the ball and his neckcloth had muffled her cries, he could still gauge their level of intensity, could hear how loud they would have been if she had not been gagged. Her ass had blushed beautifully for him. There would be more bruising this time.

His gaze fell to her breasts next. They were a lovely pair. Till now, he had not afforded them the attention they deserved, but tonight they would not be so neglected. They protruded nicely from her chest and were large enough to enable him to wrap the rope around them several times. Thus bound, her nipples extended farther than normal, and the areolas appeared disproportionately large. When she became more experienced, he might even be able to suspend her by the breasts.

He shook his head and reminded himself that this was to be their last time together.

He cupped a swollen mound. Her brows shot up, indicating how sensitive her breasts had become. Lowering his head, he licked a nipple. She whimpered.

"Are you ready to proceed?"

She nodded.

"You may lie down upon the table. On your back."

She did as he bid, wincing when her derrière came to rest

upon the top of the table. He allowed her to set her feet on the table and lift some of the weight off her aching rump.

"Show me how you pleasured yourself that night you failed to follow my orders."

She reached a hand between her thighs and stroked herself. He watched for a few minutes, feeling the blood course hot and strong through his veins. Her body begged to be fucked. But he had to finish his task. With more rope, he tied her wrists to either corners of the table by securing the rope to the legs. He noticed that she still refrained from settling down upon her arse.

"You will want to lift your backside higher," he said.

She looked at him, puzzled. From the sideboard, he retrieved two short votives he had lit earlier. He slid them beneath her, compelling her to lift her hips and arch her back. He went to light two more and added these to the table. He caressed the length of one leg, feeling the tautness of the muscles as she strained to keep her body above the candle flames.

He passed his hand over her belly, then threaded his fingers through the hairs at her mound. It would be fun to shave these ample curls, he thought to himself. There was much he would like to do to Millie, but he was limited by time.

With his forefinger, he teased the swollen bud beneath her curls. Her lashes fluttered, and she moaned when he sank an inch of his digit into her sodden slit. His cock throbbed with need, but without the use of her safety word, he would need to pay careful attention to her. He retrieved the duster and brushed it over her torso. Half gasps and chuckles escaped through the ball and linen. Her body jerked as it tried to avoid the feathers, but upon greeting the heat below, returned to its prior position. Which would be worse for her, the tickling or the burning? He knew from their time at Château Follet that she was particularly sensitive to the former, and from her struggles, she seemed to waver equally between the duster and the candles. Perspiration soon appeared upon her, lending a beautiful gloss to her body. The gasps and chuckles turned into grunts as the straining grew harder to maintain. Her body began to quiver.

Knowing she needed more air, and not wanting her to lose consciousness, he pulled the linen down to free her nose. Setting aside the duster, he put his hand to her mons and slid his finger along her clitoris. By now, her legs wanted to give in, but if she wanted the rapture of his fondling, she had to maintain her position. He lifted his hand a little higher, and her pelvis followed, seeking his touch. He played with her clitoris, rubbing it, pinching it. She panted heavily, her face brightened with perspiration. Her body, tired, did eventually sink toward the table, but shot back up when the flames licked her arse.

With both hands, he caressed her belly, her hips, her thighs, spreading the moisture over her soft skin. Her breasts had darkened in color, and he decided to release them from their bondage. After removing the rope, he bent over and encased a nipple with his mouth. She cried out loudly as her body bowed toward the table to avoid his mouth, but doing so sent her closer to the flames. She was stuck, her sensitive nipple trapped in his mouth.

She started sobbing when he sucked. She continued to cry even after he released the nipple and pushed the candles to a part of the table where the flames would not threaten her. She collapsed onto the table, and it mattered not that her buttocks were still sore. He waited till the vigor of her breathing had relaxed. He brushed a tendril of hair that had matted to her forehead. When she had calmed sufficiently, she turned to meet his gaze. With the lower half of her face covered, her eyes appeared particularly expressive and luminescent. At the moment, they were the loveliest eyes he had ever beheld.

"Do you wish to call an end to your punishment?" he asked.

Her bosom continued to heave as she drew in much-needed air, but her gaze conveyed a strength he had not expected. She shook her head.

He rolled her breasts, still dark from the blood that had been trapped there, then passed his hands over the curves and planes of her torso till his right hand reached the destination between her legs. He fondled her there, sinking two digits into her wet heat. His fingers curled, caressed and stroked, making her squirm atop the table.

"Would you care for cock now?"

She nodded.

"Are you certain?"

She nodded again.

Withdrawing his hand, he went to the sideboard and found the dildo she had wrapped her mouth about that first night. Her eyes widened, and she shook her head a little. But her body was ready. It had been craving release for nearly forty-eight hours. There was more than enough wetness to ease the dildo in.

He first rubbed the tip of the false cock against her clitoris. She moaned. When she was sufficiently aroused, he lowered the cock to her slit, but he only pressed the head in half an inch, teasing her, before sliding the dildo back to her clitoris. Soon, she bucked her hips in search of the cock and made no protest when it gained entry. But her acceptance came to a quick halt when more than an inch of the dildo began to fill her. She made a high-pitched sound and tried to evade the intruder, but her bonds kept her from moving too far.

With his free hand, he held her down at the hip. "Relax. You are capable of taking the dildo."

She inhaled several short breaths.

"Do you wish to speak your safety word?"

She considered it a moment, then shook her head.

He moved his hand from her hip to her clitoris and flicked it as his other hand pressed the dildo farther into her. She squeezed her eyes shut.

"Breathe," he reminded her, and made his own breathing audible to guide her.

She gave a stilted groan, and he could see her body still wanted an escape, but the dildo was nestled two inches deep now. He continued to toy with her clitoris till arousal superseded the discomfort of having the large dildo stretching her cunnie.

"Ungh," she panted several times.

"Breathe. You're doing supremely well, Millie."

Four inches.

He increased his fondling of her clitoris. Her eyes rolled towards the back of her head. The dildo might now contribute to the pleasure. Her toes curled.

Six inches.

He could sense her cunnie clenching down upon the cock. Some women came to enjoy large cocks, and he suspected Millie might be one of them. Two more inches and the cock would be completely inside her.

"Millie, you are a wonder," he encouraged.

She whimpered in response. He rubbed her clitoris vigorously. He could feel the tension of her impending orgasm rising in her body.

It was done.

Her cunnie had swallowed the whole of the large dildo.

"Well done!" he praised.

To complete her punishment, he took two of the candles and hovered them over her body. She squirmed at their nearness. Raising the candles, he tilted them to allow the liquid wax to fall upon her. She struggled against the ropes that held her as hot wax splattered over her ribs, her belly, and her mound. Her body became a canvas for him to decorate, and when little remained of the candles, he stepped back to admire his artwork.

My God, she was beautiful.

His own cock had waited long enough. Removing his banyan and nightshirt, he straddled her body atop the table. He eyed her lush breasts and positioned his shaft between them. He pressed the orbs together about his cock. Her mouth and cunnie were superior, but he would enjoy fucking her teats. There was not a part of Millie he did not relish.

He pumped his hips a few times before reaching over and untying the ropes from her wrists. She knew what to do, and pushed her breasts together. Not having to hold her orbs in place allowed him more freedom of motion. He quickened his pace, gliding his stiffness between the spheres. Desire, boiling in his cods, sought its long-awaited release. He glanced back to see that the dildo was still in place, and the thought of that mass filling and stretching her cunnie sent him over the edge. His hips bucked wildly as his seed shot forth, spraying her throat and collar.

When he withdrew from her breasts, his cock throbbed still as more of his mettle pulsed from its tip. His body gave a violent shudder. He stroked himself as the ecstasy inside him settled from a riot to a simmer. And he had not thought the rapture of the previous night could be surpassed. When the currents shivering through his limbs had dissipated, he pulled down the neckcloth and removed the collar and ball from her mouth.

"Thank you, my lord," she mustered, though her mouth was undoubtedly sore.

"You were marvelous," he said, then climbed off the table. "You took your punishment well, and for that, you shall be rewarded. How would you like to spend?"

He looked over her body, adorned with the candlewax and his drying seed. He reached for her mons.

"May I request a different reward, my lord?"

Surprised, he wondered what she could possibly want more. Retribution, perhaps?

"Such as?"

"I have a greater wish. I would rather you not give your ready support to Farnsworth till you have thoroughly examined the arguments against his bill."

He stared at her, stunned. Was this truly what she preferred? It was highly irregular. Outlandish, even.

"Millie, our carnal pursuits do not involve politics."

"Why not? You forbade me to talk of stocking frames as part of our arrangement. It would seem there is nothing that *you* cannot involve."

He had to acknowledge her reasoning, but still he could not completely believe what she was asking. After all that her body had endure, it surely needed release. She deserved to spend.

"Are you certain this is what you want?" he asked.

She nodded.

A strange emotion overwhelmed him. Of awe and even shame. She was unlike any woman he had ever known.

"I will consider it," he said finally. "I do not owe Farnsworth my support. Nevertheless, I will only promise to delay my decision."

"That is all I ask."

His hand was between her legs, an area too much the temptation despite her request. He stroked her nub with his middle finger. She moaned softly.

"Pray do not tease me further, my lord."

"Shhhh."

He continued to fondle her. She bit her lower lip but eventually released a moan when his fingers found the spot of greatest sensitivity.

"Alastair—my lord, you will make me spend. Oh, G—no." She gripped the edge of the table with both hands. "*Please.*"

He was accustomed to hearing submissives begging to spend, but Millie begged *not* to spend. Perhaps because he had not explicitly granted her permission, but he intended she should.

"My lord—ah—ah!"

After caging her desire for two days, her body could not resist the temptation.

"Spend, Millie," he commanded.

Her body fell into convulsions, rattling the table below. Her hips bucked a few times before settling back down when he eased his strokes. She panted for a different purpose now.

"I was sincere in my request for a different reward," she bemoaned when the trembling had quieted.

"And you will have it."

He walked to the foot of the table and swiped the candles to the floor before setting himself between her legs. He eyed the handle of the dildo protruding from her.

"How does your cunnie enjoy the cock?" he asked.

"I'm not sure," she murmured.

He pulled the dildo out an inch, then two, before pushing it back in. She grunted. Lowering himself, he licked at her clitoris. He applied his tongue to her in earnest.

"Oh, God. What is it you wish, my lord? You cannot…"

Encasing her bud of desire, he sucked, liking the taste of her. The scent of her arousal caused his lust to swell.

"May I, my lord?" she managed through clenched teeth.

He moved the dildo in and out of her as he continued to assault her with his mouth.

"Ah! I beg of you. Let me spend."

Her body quivered. He released her long enough to give his assent. Her response was immediate. Her body bowed off

the table. Her legs kicked against the bonds, a thigh knock-
ing into the side of his head. Her scream made him consider
that he had prematurely removed her gag. But it was exhil-
arating to see, hear and feel her body succumb to euphoria.

He kept her aloft at the apex till she cried for him to cease.
She sobbed for breath. His cock stretched, yearning to mate
to her, but it could not compare to the dildo currently occu-
pying the envied place. Though there was another orifice
he would have liked to penetrate, but he would not task her
further tonight.

CHAPTER TWENTY-THREE

———◇◈◇◈◇———

THE CEILING STILL BLURRED BEFORE her eyes. Mildred marveled that her body had survived the second orgasm. Alastair had applied his mouth *there* and allowed her to spend, despite her willingness not to. Had it all been a test? Had she failed it? But it did not matter. This was their last night together. Ever. She closed her eyes and drank in the splendor still waving through her body.

"Thank you, my lord. Thank you."

Gently, he eased the false cock from her. She was relieved to have it gone. The infernal thing had stretched her most uncomfortably, though, when Alastair had fondled her, its presence had aided in her arousal.

"At Château Follet, there are dildos twice this size," he said.

"Dear God. Such largeness must split a woman in twain."

"The cunnie can accommodate much more than you would expect. Whole fists—"

"Whole fists!"

Her mind whirled. There was so much of Château Follet left to explore. But she was not to go there. She had promised him she would not.

Setting aside the dildo, he caressed the muscles in her legs. They had never worked this hard. Now that desire had receded, the less pleasurable consequences of her torment returned to various parts of her body. After untying the ropes from her ankles, he cleansed her body, removing the dried wax and wiping his seed from her. As she sat atop the table upon her tender derrière, he passed the wet linen over her breasts. She relished the way he gazed at her bosom, at his touch upon her body. At times, she forgot that she had a body of middling beauty.

He went to pour her a glass of ratafia, and she realized she was quite thirsty. After she finished the beverage, he assisted her down, but her legs, fatigued from their earlier exertions, gave way beneath her weight. He caught her. Feeling her breasts brush against him, his arms about her sent a wave of warmth surging through her. He seemed to sense it, for his cock perked. She looked up at him. She did not want the night to end.

His lips crushed down upon hers, and it was as if she had not spent twice already. Her arousal never tired in his presence. Despite her shaky legs, she tried to press herself to him as she wrapped her hands about his neck to help hold herself up. Sweeping her into his arms, he carried her to a mattress in the corner. Compared to the table, the mattress stuffed with straw was as soft as down.

Laying himself over her, he resumed kissing her, taking her mouth with bruising fervor. She gripped his hair in one hand and his shoulder in the other. Her hips met his body, seeking his erection. She was overcome with impatience and wanted his body to meld into hers. He ground himself against her as his mouth ravaged hers.

"I should search for French letters," he uttered against her lips.

Not bearing to be parted from him, she wrapped a leg over his and tightened her embrace. "Take me, my lord. Take me."

It was an invitation he could not refuse. He positioned his

cock at her opening and plunged in. Though she had been stretched by the dildo, his cock felt no less grand. The angle and shape of his shaft provoked much more pleasure. She pushed herself down on him, wanting every inch.

"My God, Millie," he breathed, groping one of her breasts.

Gradually, they came to a rhythm with their bodies. Holding the bottom of a thigh, he lifted the leg to gain deeper penetration. Lust overcame the soreness of her legs, the tenderness of her backside, and she shoved herself up at him. He met her fervor and rolled his hips into her, sending waves of delight fanning from between her legs. She grunted and babbled half words, trying to resist the tide of pleasure threatening to drown her.

"Spend. As you please, my lord," she managed, digging her fingers into his muscular arms.

"Ladies first," he replied.

At this, her body shattered. He cupped his hand over her mouth to dampen her cries. Her body bucked of its own accord. He quickened his pace, hammering himself into her till his own release became eminent. He pulled from her as his seed shot into the mattress below. To her consternation and slight trepidation, she would rather he had spent inside her. Several shivers went through his frame.

"Oh my! I'm terribly sorry," she gasped when she saw that her fingers—and nails—had dug into him harder than she had realized

He glanced at the scratches upon his upper arm. "It is nothing. I once had a woman draw blood with her teeth."

She wished he would remain where he was, the weight of his body resting partially upon her, but he pushed himself up and held out his hand to her. Their evening had come to an end.

"Thank you, Alastair. Thank you for the past three nights."

"I pray they met your expectations?"

"Mmmmm. Exceeded expectations."

"Good."

He turned her around to inspect her rump. "You will have bruises. Madame Follet had a poultice that would quicken the healing. Perhaps Katherine—"

"Oh, no! She must not know."

"She knew what transpired betwixt us before."

"Yes, but, in her house—I could not. She would think me a glutton, and, as I have already erred—pray, I will be fine. May I assist you in tidying the room?"

"The bedclothes upon the mattress will need to be washed."

She nodded. "I shall see to it somehow."

In silence, they placed all the implements and candles back in order. Dressed, they surveyed the room, the scene of three nights she would never forget.

"Alastair, I cannot thank you enough."

"The pleasure was mine."

She hoped he spoke sincerely and not merely from courtesy. She reminded herself that he was not a man compelled by obligations of the latter.

"Good night, Millie."

"Good night."

As she strolled down the corridor toward the stairs, a mix of feelings beset her. She felt both a euphoria and guilt, shame at what she had done, what she had asked of her cousin, but gratitude that he had acquiesced in taking her to such sublime carnal heights that all future attempts must surely disappoint.

Thus, she wondered at the wisdom of her actions. However, if she had to do it all again, she would not have asked differently. She had expected nothing but punishment tonight and was thus amazed when Alastair had brought her to spend thrice.

And, additionally, he had agreed to reserve his support of

the Farnsworth bill. It was entirely possible his delay of support would be of minimal duration, even a day at most, for she had required no particular timing to her request. But while Alastair often held the expectations of polite society with contempt, she had never known him to go back on his word. He did not trifle with tricks, artifice, or even insincerity.

He was a different man than she had known before. There was no one like him to her, and she felt privileged to know a side of him few others saw.

CHAPTER TWENTY-FOUR

M ILDRED WINCED AS SHE TOOK a seat before the vanity the following morning.

"Are you all right, miss?" asked the dressing maid.

"Yes," Mildred answered as she positioned her rump to avoid the tenderest spots and not aggravate the soreness between her thighs. Her cheeks warmed as the memories of the prior night flooded her. She observed her reflection in the looking glass and noticed her plaits had come undone. She had slept soundly last night, but there were faint half circles beneath her eyes. Nonetheless, she felt buoyed by all that had transpired. She reminded herself to see that the bedclothes from the mattress were washed. Alastair had taken them to the laundry that awaited the servants.

The redness from where the ropes had bound her breasts had disappeared. Last night, the redness had peered just above the décolletage of her shift, and upon returning to her chambers, she had passed the open door of Mr. and Mrs. Wilmington's room. She had heard movement and saw the light of a candle approach, and had scurried to her room. Whoever it was, she did not think they had seen her.

When she was dressed and went downstairs, she found that everyone else had already finished breakfast except for Edward's boys. Alastair and Kittredge were already in their riding clothes.

"Miss Abbott," said Kittredge, approaching her, "I had hoped to have the chance to bid farewell. I quite enjoyed meeting you and your family. Perhaps our paths will cross back in London."

She smiled and expressed a similar sentiment. Alastair did not approach her, and she was partially glad for it. She had protested what awkwardness may come of their affair at Château Follet. But this time felt different. She wished she had not slept quite so late that she might have more of his company before he and Kittredge departed.

As Alastair accepted the well wishes from his family, Millie felt his gaze upon her often.

"I mean to host Christmas dinner," said Lady Katherine. "You will come, will you not, Andre?"

He frowned.

"Of course I will not expect you," she said, "but you are welcome, nonetheless."

Everyone moved outside to watch the two men out to their horses. Mildred assumed the appearance of indifference but found herself grappling with a sadness as she observed them depart. And when everyone returned indoors, she was the last to follow.

During what felt like a somber breakfast, she tried to rid herself of the strange sentiments that had settled upon her. She told herself that she might not see Alastair again, not for some time. And it ought not matter to her. He had gifted her three nights of ecstasy; she should expect no more from him. He was probably relieved to be done with her.

After breakfast, she declared that she would go out and enjoy the weather before winter made such outings difficult.

"I will join you for a stroll about the grounds, Miss Abbott."

Mildred turned around in surprise, for it was Mrs. Wilmington who spoke. Though she would have preferred the chance to be alone with her thoughts and feelings, she gave a short curtsy and waited till Mrs. Wilmington had donned her coat, bonnet and gloves.

They walked in silence until they were far enough from the house not to be beset by anyone. From Mrs. Wilmington's demeanor, Mildred suspected she had not joined her for friendly conversation.

"Though your standing in society differs greatly from ours," Mrs. Wilmington began, "you are, nonetheless, joined to the d'Aubigne name, which has generations of breeding."

"It is an illustrious name," Mildred acknowledged.

"You must know the importance, therefore, of acting in proper accordance with your family's elevated position. You must now adhere to higher standards."

"I shall strive to, madam, and am most sorry that my recent behavior was not in concert with expectations."

Mrs. Wilmington narrowed her eyes. "You took great liberties in your speech."

"And I am most sorry for it."

"Andre ought to have put you in your place with the harshest of words."

"Yes, I wish he had."

"The Andre I know would have spared nothing, regardless of your sex. That he did not is curious. But when you pair that with the excessive dowry he has granted you, I can only conclude that you have influenced him as only a jezebel could."

Mildred stopped in her tracks.

Mrs. Wilmington looked at her squarely. "I know what you are about, Miss Abbott."

Mildred felt her color rise. Her voice quivered when she spoke. "Madam?"

"I mean to warn you that you will only ruin yourself if you continue in the manner of a trollop. Imagine the shame your mother and father would face. It would not matter then that your uncle had married our aunt. A d'Aubigne can weather scandal, but the same cannot be said for an Abbott. Whatever your designs upon my brother—"

"I must protest, madam! I have no designs upon your brother."

"No? It was merely coincidence that you returned to your chambers shortly before Alastair did? It is more than curious that you two were both awake at such an ungodly hour."

Stunned, Mildred could make no reply. Her legs trembled beneath her skirts. When she finally found her voice, she said, "It would seem that *three* of us were awake, and perhaps it is thus not so curious."

"Your breeding shows in your impudence, Miss Abbott. I know that I suffer from insomnia. Can you say the same?"

"It was a coincidence."

"That you would attempt to deny it only sinks you further in my estimation."

Mildred looked away. What was she to do? What could she say?

"But I will keep your dirty secret if you can assure me that you will cease this jezebel business. I have long deplored Andre's profligacy, but with Lady Sophia, there is hope that his indulgent ways will finally come to an end."

"Madam, I can assure you that you need have no worries. You are mistaken in your presumptions. There is nothing between Alastair and I."

Mrs. Wilmington raised a single brow. "I presume that you are a light-skirt, and that Andre, being the man that he is, does not hesitate to make use of such easy virtue. If you were not in Katherine's good graces, you should be no different than a whore that he would take to bed before casting back into the streets."

The constriction in her chest made responding difficult.

"If I were you," Mrs. Wilmington continued, "I would

make use of your dowry whilst you have it, and marry the first man who offers. Perhaps he will never discover the doxy that you are. Andre will succumb to his obligations. He has enough pride in the d'Aubigne name that he will not shirk his duties. He many continue his dalliances even after marrying Lady Sophia, as many men are wont to do, but if you have any fanciful notions that he will favor you, you have but to look at his pattern of behavior. I could let you descend into disgrace—it is a fate you most assuredly deserve—but you have the chance to save yourself and your family from utter ruin. If you have any decency in you, you will take my advice."

Without another word, she turned and headed back to the house.

Still in shock, Mildred stood without moving. When Mrs. Wilmington was no longer in view, Mildred reached for the nearest tree and sank to the ground beside it. Her chest hurt, the pain exceeding any she had experienced last night at Alastair's hands.

It ought not matter what Mrs. Wilmington thought of her, but it did. Because she was Alastair's sister and Lady Katherine's niece. But Mildred knew there was little she could do to earn the good graces of Mrs. Wilmington. She did not doubt that the woman could carry out her threat, though she need not have worried. Mildred would not have wanted to harm the d'Aubigne family in any way. She respected Lady Katherine too much.

And she loved Alastair.

CHAPTER TWENTY-FIVE

"AS LONG AS SLAVERY IS safe in the colonies, the economies there need not collapse," Mr. Carleton explained at the dinner table. "It was more economical to import slaves than to encourage them to breed. A slave's first five years are useless and a burdensome cost to the slave owner, but now that the slave trade has been abolished, we have little choice. That is why you have seen the price of sugar rise, Mrs. Abbott."

Mildred bit her tongue to keep from speaking, telling herself that doing so would only prolong the conversation. She kept her attention upon the partridge on her plate.

"And are you quite certain you must travel to the West Indies in December?" her mother asked. "Why, you will likely have to spend Christmas aboard a ship!"

"Alas, our plantation manager is gravely ill, and quite possibly dead as we speak. I would, of course, much rather spend Christmas here in England."

Mildred felt his gaze upon her.

"Well, when you are returned, we shall certainly have to have you over once more for a proper welcoming dinner."

"I hope you will spend Christmas more enjoyably than I?"

"We will have Christmas dinner with Lady Katherine, the aunt of the Marquess of Alastair. We spent Michaelmas with her at her country estate."

"I remember. What a fine family are the d'Aubignes. They have an illustrious history."

"Yes, and they will soon join with the equally exalted family, the Strathingtons, for we expect a betrothal between the Marquess of Alastair and Lady Sophia."

"Indeed? Felicitations on such a grand union for your families."

This was not the first that Mildred had heard of Alastair and Lady Sophia recently, and she was determined not to be forlorn.

Since Michaelmas, her mother had redoubled her efforts to obtain an offer of marriage for Mildred, and Mildred had considered choosing one simply so that she would no longer have to entertain Mr. Carleton and Mr. Porter. The one gentleman whose company she did welcome was that of George Winston. If not for him, she would've found herself thinking too often of Alastair in the months since Michaelmas. She had kept herself busy and spent much more time with friends than she used to do. Though for several weeks after, she could not pass the day without thinking of him, and at night, her body burned for his touch, eventually she could face the memory of him without the pain of sadness. She had even declined two invitations from Lady Katherine, for his aunt would remind her too much of him.

"ARE YOU QUITE CERTAIN YOU don't want to go to the club for cards?" Kittredge asked as he and Alastair guided their horses past the trees in the field outside of London. "The manager had me sample some Russian spirits. I know they are not quite the gentlemanly drink but I rather liked their potency."

Alastair observed the gray clouds in the sky. There was

likely to be rain, and if they rode much longer, they might be caught in a shower, but part of him would not mind. Ever since returning from Edenmoor, he had wanted to be out of doors as often as possible. The brisk autumn air helped to calm his ardor whenever his thoughts turned to Millie.

He had erred in agreeing to her proposition yet again. Only this time, it would be harder to shake the spell she had cast upon him. He appreciated that she had made no effort to contact him in the fortnights following Michaelmas. Too many women entertained hopes that he would renew their acquaintance despite his advice to the contrary. Millie was far too practical for such fancies. She knew that if he wanted her company, he would seek her out, and not expect to receive a letter or visit from her.

And yet, when his butler brought him each day's mail, Alastair found himself looking for a letter from Millie. At night especially, and even during the day when there were far more distractions to be had, his mind would wander back to Edenmoor. To the bright crimson of her ass after the paddling. To the triumph shining in her eyes when she had caused him to spend in her mouth. To the glow of rapture upon her countenance after her body had succumbed to his ministrations. There was no better triumph or accomplishment than making a woman spend. Millie especially. He often considered what more he could do with her. The possibilities were endless.

"Then perhaps you will join me at the club tomorrow evening," offered Kittredge.

"Alas, I am to escort the Duchess and Lady Sophia to a pantomime tomorrow," Alastair replied.

"Ah, I had meant to ask about Lady Sophia. You have been seen in her company more often, and I have been asked by our friend, Sir Carrie, how he should bet at Brooks's. When is an announcement expected?"

Alastair had thought that spending more time with Lady Sophia would help to ease away the memories of Millie, but he only found himself comparing the two women. Without doubt, Lady Sophia, with her golden curls, long thick lashes, and alabaster complexion, was a beauty none could rival. And she was perfectly aware of this; thus, she carried herself with a regal confidence that Millie would never have. Their stations in life could not be more different. The daughter of a Duke, Lady Sophia had all the connections anyone could want in society. Millie clearly had not, yet she still had much compassion in her heart. He was still astounded that, when given the chance to enjoy her much deserved euphoria, she had chosen instead to ask for his consideration on behalf of weavers. What woman would propose such nonsense? It had been clear her body needed and desired to spend. Her request was tangential, even if admirably selfless. It was not the sort of proposition he would ever had made, which explained his surprise and awe.

Realizing that he had been silent, and that his silence had earned the careful study of his friend, Alastair said, "And did you advise Sir Carrie how he should place his bet?"

"I told Carrie that I am not privy to your innermost thoughts. We share wine and cards, but not women. I did say, however, that you have had more than ample time to ask for Lady Sophia's hand, and despite your reputation, His Grace is amenable to you for a son-in-law. That an announcement has not been forthcoming marks some hesitation on your part, I think. But Carrie responded that you are loath to do what others expect of you, and I had to agree there was much truth in that. Would you consider my assessment a fair one?"

"It is as Carrie says: my actions are not guided by what others wish to see from me. When I am ready to propose to Lady Sophia, you may be assured that you will be the first to know."

As he spoke, he wondered if you would be ever ready to ask for her hand in marriage.

"Will I know far enough in advance to place a bet myself?" Kittredge asked.

As Kittredge spoke in jest, Alastair made no answer, though he would not put it above Kittredge to use his position of friendship to monetary advantage.

They rode in silence for a spell before Kittredge said, "Shall I have the pleasure of meeting your cousin again?"

Alastair stiffened. "My cousin?"

"Miss Abbott. She is quite the interesting creature. She seems so deferential to the likes of your aunt, your sisters, and her parents. I would almost say she is a shy young woman, but she speaks to you with a daring few women would."

Millie did address him with much more ease than she did others, which was odd because she ought to have found him far more intimidating than the individuals Kittredge had named. Alastair found her audacity both vexing and impressive.

"Perhaps she does not hold you in much esteem," Kittredge mused, "and that is why she finds such courage to address you as she does."

Alastair would have to agree that that was likely how it started for Millie, but he hoped that she had come to find more reason to value his thoughts and opinions despite their disagreements.

"My aunt no doubt encourages her boldness," Alastair replied dryly.

"I can fathom why your aunt might be partial to her. She is not much to look at upon first glance and not the cleverest in conversation, but there is definitely a quality to her that compels, the more one is acquainted with her."

"And what is your purpose in talking of Miss Abbott?"

"No purpose at all. She merely popped into my mind by happenstance."

Alastair let that be the end of their dialogue and started his horse into a full gallop.

CHAPTER TWENTY-SIX

M RS. ABBOTT LOOKED OUT THE window of the drawing room and frowned. She sniffed, "It's that George Winston fellow again."

Mildred tied her bonnet in place and smiled to herself. It was the one name her mother had recently uttered that did not cause her to cringe.

"Why is he so often with the Grenvilles? And they have Harold Wiggins with them," Mrs. Abbott continued. "I wonder that Wiggins has a farthing to his name? His family is practically penniless if you take into account all the debts his father has. No doubt four thousand pounds would mean a great deal to him."

"No doubt," agreed Mildred, "but despite that, he is most interested in Jane. I could have a dowry of ten thousand pounds, and he would not look my way."

Mrs. Abbot sniffed again. "Well, that simply shows that he lacks sense as well! And what of Winston? What do we know of his situation?"

"I gather he is well situated enough, but it hardly matters. I do not think him overly partial to me. Not when he has the attentions of Miss Hannah Rose."

That piece of intelligence seemed to appease Mrs. Abbott a little. She knew that Mr. and Mrs. Rose would never permit their daughter to favor a man with no standing.

"Nevertheless, it would be more worth your while to keep the company of some others. Mr. Carleton, for example, has requested to speak with your father on his return. I expect the topic of conversation will be a *proposal*."

"Mr. Carleton reeks of tobacco and has a propensity to pick his teeth when he thinks no one is looking."

"What does that matter? He is a far better prospect than someone like Winston."

"It is not only income that makes for a good husband."

"We are of a family with the d'Aubignes. It is your obligation to wed well or your dowry is gone to waste."

Mrs. Abbott had been in particular good spirits ever since Michaelmas. An invitation to dine with Lady Katherine for Christmas had only added to her glee.

"Take care you do not give Winston any encouragement," her mother advised after Mildred bid her adieu.

Although modesty had prompted Mildred to say to her mother that Mr. Winston took only a cursory interest in her, she suspected it was not the case. And if he should show greater interest, she did not think she would discourage him as her mother wanted.

"I saw this pantomime last year," said Jane after they had entered the Theatre Royal, "and I thought it quite amusing, especially Clown."

"What of you, Miss Abbott?" asked Mr. Winston. "Do you enjoy pantomimes?"

"I do," Mildred answered.

"Look there," Jane whispered to Mildred. "There is Miss Rose. She sees us, and is not at all happy to see Mr. Winston is in our company. You should vex her further by flirting with Mr. Winston."

Mildred opened her mouth to object, but the words never came out, for she saw Alastair across the room. He had on his arm a most beautiful woman, with golden locks framing a sweet face comprising a charming nose and dainty, rosy lips.

"See there," said Mr. Grenville, "is that your cousin, Miss Abbott?"

"And I think the woman to be Lady Sophia, daughter of a Duke," added Mrs. Grenville.

"How lovely she is!" said Jane.

"Are they betrothed yet?" asked Mrs. Grenville.

"I know not," replied Millie after a difficult swallow. "But I think there is much talk of it."

"What a grand wedding they must have! How lucky you are, Millie, for certainly you will receive an invitation."

Alastair and the woman were headed to the boxes and did not seem to see her. Mildred tried not to look up at the balconies where they would be sitting, but during the entire performance, her mind traveled to where her gaze avoided. She pretended to enjoy the pantomime far more than she did. At one point, she gasped in surprise when Clown surprised Harlequin from a trap door. She inadvertently grabbed for the arm of her chair, only to land her hand upon Mr. Winston's. She blushed. He returned a warm smile.

"I once saw an actor, in the role of Clown, leap from a platform above the stage, rotate in the air, and land on his feet," Mr. Winston said.

They talked about some of the most daring and comic stunts they had seen, but Mildred admitted that as much as she enjoyed the pantomime, she favored dramas much more.

"Tragedies or comedies?" he asked.

She considered the answer. "What think you?"

"Tragedies."

"You know me well, Mr. Winston."

"Given I had but two choices, the odds were pretty good for me."

They shared a laugh.

During the interval, Mr. Winston and Mr. Wiggins offered to purchase lemonade and confections for the women. Shortly after they returned, Jane bid them fetch some fruits, for she wanted to speak with Mildred while they strolled the lobby.

"I think my father would approve of Mr. Wiggins," Jane confided. "He is a good sort of man, though he is not so rich as my family would wish, but they desire my happiness."

"How fortunate for you, Jane! I agree that Mr. Wiggins is a fine man, and I would that more parents thought as liberally as your father," Mildred replied.

"What thinks your father of Mr. Winston?"

"My mother does not consider him—"

"Miss Abbott."

Mildred felt her heart stop in mid-beat. She turned around to face the Marquess. He bowed coolly to Jane before saying, "May I have a word, Miss Abbott?"

Seeing that the Marquess appeared unhappy, Jane did a quick curtsy and scurried away as if fleeing for her life. Mildred looked for Lady Sophia but did not see her.

"My lord," Mildred said, "how are you enjoying the—"

He interrupted, "What are you doing in the company of that man?"

Taken aback by his brusque tone, she asked, "What man?"

"That Winston fellow. I knew him at Oxford."

"He is a friend of the Grenville family."

"You should avoid his company."

"Why? He is an amiable and thoughtful gentleman."

"You thought the same of the Viscount Devon."

"And I still have no evidence to think otherwise."

"You have my advice."

"And why do you advise against Mr. Winston?"

"I do not recall the specifics, but there was some sort of affair involving him and a young woman of little standing."

"I did not think you easily persuaded by rumors."

"This was no rumor."

"It would seem a common accusation of young men at Oxford to have had dalliances, and whatever happened, this was many years ago."

"I somewhat doubt that he is significantly changed for the better. What transpired spoke to a serious flaw of character."

"And what was it that transpired?"

"He was not of my year, and I spared it little heed, but as wretched as I am, I did not think highly of him after what I had heard."

"When you have recalled what had happened or what you had heard, I will hear what you have to say. Till then—"

"Till then, you will not entertain his company."

She bristled. "You are not my father."

"I am the one providing your dowry."

"Which you can dispense with at any time."

She saw a muscle in his jaw tighten.

"Are you often in his company?"

"You are impertinent, Alastair."

"He must be attracted to your dowry if he seeks your company."

She fumed that he would suggest her company was not worth seeking if not for her dowry. "Then he would be no different than every man who seeks me out! And it is your fault for granting me such a dowry."

He pressed his lips into a grim line before saying, "You invited my involvement with that Haversham fellow. I will approve whomever you wish to marry."

"And what if I wish to marry Mr. Winston?"

"I would sooner you wed Kittredge, and he is no good for any woman."

At that moment, the orchestra began, indicating the performance was about to resume.

"There you are, Miss Abbott." Mr. Winston had approached. Upon seeing Alastair, he made a stiff bow. "Lord Alastair, you may not recall but we were at Oxford together."

"I do recall, Mr. Winston," Alastair responded, his face darkening.

A brief and awkward silence followed.

"I think we should take our seats," Mildred said to Mr. Winston. She made a curtsy to Alastair.

As she and Mr. Winston returned to their seats with the Grenvilles and Wiggins, he observed, "I do not think your cousin pleased to see me."

"He is cross with everyone," Mildred answered, her mind half turned to what Alastair had said.

"Perhaps he recalls the less encouraging moments of my time at Oxford. I was more foolish then, frequented one too many taverns and fell in love far too often. There was one young woman in particular. She and I had become exceedingly fond of one another, but, alas, she had no connections, and my family would not approve our marriage. It broke my heart to tell her that we could not marry, and I considered it all quite my fault. She was younger and more naive. The tragedy of it is that she took her own life not long after, and I shall carry the burden of my actions to my grave."

He lowered his head.

"I am sorry to hear it," Mildred said, moved by his sadness.

"I should have known better, and been the party of greater responsibility, but I have learned from my mistakes. I am much more careful of falling in love now."

"That you place the blame upon yourself shows tremendous character," she praised, and put a hand upon his arm.

He looked at her with gratitude. "I do not deserve your compliments, Miss Abbott. Not on this matter."

Her heart ached for his pain. Alastair had merely assumed

the worst of Mr. Winston, and, given his own shortcomings, he ought not cast stones so readily at others.

Alastair's attempts to interfere in her life suddenly, when he had made no attempt to see her after Michaelmas, rankled her for reasons she knew not why. She certainly did not appreciate his overbearing manner in forbidding her continued acquaintance with Mr. Winston. While she had played a submissive to Alastair at Château Follet and Edenmoor, she was *not* his constant submissive to be ordered about.

At the end of the performance, as he was with Lady Sophia, Millie was, to her relief, spared from having to speak with the Marquess again. As her party stood outside awaiting their carriage, Mildred and Mr. Winston chanced to stand a little ways from Wiggins, Jane, and her parents.

"Mr. Winston, Miss Abbott," greeted Hannah Rose, who had ventured a few steps from her family to greet them. "Miss Abbott, I rarely see you at the theater. What brings you here tonight?"

"The Grenvilles have made it a tradition to see the pantomime at Christmas each year," Mildred replied. "I am a guest of theirs."

Miss Rose showed no interest in her answer and had already begun addressing Mr. Winston. "Did you enjoy the pantomime?"

"I did," Mr. Winston replied politely.

"The view is much better from the boxes. My family has an annual subscription. Perhaps I can persuade my father to extend you an invitation."

Mr. Winston made no reply. Miss Rose was recalled by her family, for their carriage had arrived.

"Am I ungrateful if I feel relieved that her family has not extended such an invitation?" Mr. Winston asked quietly.

"There may be men who would call you that, for the attentions of Miss Rose are quite coveted," Mildred said.

"I suppose, but I seek more in a woman than wealth or beauty. My family wishes I were not so particular. They are quite anxious for me to wed."

"As are mine," Mildred sighed.

"I think I cannot forbear them longer. At times I have been tempted to simply marry the first woman I see, but I cannot be content with a woman lest I hold her in regard. She must be easy to converse with, like you, and of an easy disposition."

Mildred was struck with an inspiration. "I dare say, and you may find this presumptuous—ridiculous even—and I will take no offense if you should think it precisely that. But, as you and I are in similar situations, perhaps we could find a solution that would eliminate the pressures we both face."

His countenance brightened. "I am intrigued, Miss Abbott."

"As we seem to find each other's company pleasurable, have no dearth of topics to converse on, share similar sensibilities, perhaps it would not be so farfetched a notion if we were to wed one another."

"Do you truly think so, Miss Abbott?" he cried.

"I do."

"And I think we should deal with each other famously! Should I drop to bended knee here?"

"Oh no! That would not do. You ought to speak to my father first."

"Will he give his consent?"

"He might, if he is not too persuaded by my mother. She wishes me to wed a man of great income."

"As she should. She wants security for her daughter. But I will have my family write to her to explain that I am more than capable of providing for all that you need and more."

Mildred felt giddy. She had not expected to find a man as handsome and charming as Mr. Winston who might also be partial to her. Alastair, if he maintained his opinion of Mr. Winston, would not approve the match, but the worst he could do was revoke her dowry, which she had never truly desired from him in the first place.

"I shall come by to speak to your father on Thursday, shall I?"

"Yes, yes."

Jane called to them then. As they rode the carriage home, Mr. Winston sat opposite Mildred. They exchanged several smiles. The carriage stopped at Mildred's house first, and Mr. Winston insisted upon walking her to the door.

"Till Thursday," he said, kissing her hand as a servant opened the door.

"Yes, Thursday," said Mildred, a little breathless. "Good night, Mr. Winston."

"How was the pantomime?" Mr. Abbott asked when the Grenville carriage had departed.

"Amusing,"

"Is that all?"

"The costumes were brilliantly colorful, and the actress playing Columbine was quite talented in her role."

She spoke with calm, but inside she was hardly serene. Alastair may not approve of Mr. Winston, but Mr. Winston was her best chance for matrimonial bliss.. Mr. Winston could have wooed the willing Miss Rose, but he had always chosen different company, and Mildred believed the man had a genuine interest for her. She could hardly wait for Thursday.

CHAPTER TWENTY-SEVEN

———◇◇◇———

"I KNEW GEORGE WINSTON WELL DURING our time at Oxford," said the gentleman, Henry Stanton. He and Alastair stood at the billiard table at one of the gentlemen's clubs on the Strand. "But I have not been in contact with him since then."

"If you do not deem it too prying, I should like to hear all that you know of him," said Alastair.

Stanton aimed his cue stick at one of the billiard balls. "I considered him a good friend at the time, but we parted ways after an unfortunate affair."

"I recall some matter with a young woman, Miss Jones. I would say he took her maidenhead, but I think his involvement entailed far worse."

"Yes. There was quite the scene, for she had come to the campus in search of him and, finding him on one of the lawns, proceeded to speak to him before no small number of persons. She was not a person of much consequence but very pretty. George had lain with her a few times, and it led to her being with child. She came to plead for his assistance, for her family had thrown her out."

Alastair watched the ball strike a skittle. "Was it certain the child was his?"

"The lass was a virgin. George complained of the copious amount of blood she shed when he took her maidenhead.

She fancied herself in love with him, and he with her. I doubt she would have lain with another."

"I understand that Winston received her rather coldly."

Stanton nodded and stood aside as Alastair took his turn. "He was, in my humble opinion, surprisingly callous. He responded that she was mistaken. And how dare she impugn his character. It seemed he could not rid himself of her presence fast enough. He spoke with such vitriol, and the poor thing looked so devastated, I would have intervened had I no loyalty to George at the time. I approached her afterward and offered what money I had on me. I implored George to take some pity upon the creature. He need not marry her, but perhaps he could provide some funding for her. He would not, and claimed that she had entrapped him. Her misery evoked no sympathy from him. A few days later, she leaped off the edge of a cliff to her death."

"Did he show any remorse for what happened?"

"I cannot say for certain. After I had expressed my disappointment in his actions, he no longer desired my company. I regret that I had not cautioned the young lady against George. He had always talked of marrying an heiress, and I knew his dalliance with the young woman was nothing more than a lark to him."

"I hope he is a changed man, and that the years have afforded him more wisdom and charity."

"What I had heard gives me little hope. A mutual acquaintance had mentioned his attempts to woo the daughter of a nabob, but the father deemed him unworthy, for he had no income and lived off an inheritance from his uncle. George had then attempted to seduce the girl into a compromising situation, forcing the father's hand, but when the family got wind of it, they sent her off to a nunnery. George is charming, to be sure, and amiable company for both sexes. But, upon examination of our time together, there had always been evidence of a selfishness that I had failed to see. Even if he has improved in the years since I have known, had I a daughter, I would not permit her within several yards of him."

When they had finished the round of billiards, Alastair thanked the man for the game and his time. He left the club and ordered his driver to Cheapside, where the Abbotts lived. If they were not at home, he would wait for them. What he had observed of Millie and Winston last night at the theater did not bode well. And once again she had seemed dismissive of his cautions.

Alastair found the Abbotts at home, and the most surprised and flustered Mrs. Abbott was the first to greet him. She said that Mr. Abbott would be down shortly, as he was just waking from his nap. When Mildred appeared, equally surprised as her mother to see him, Mrs. Abbott snapped at her daughter to bring tea as quickly as she could.

"Pray, have a seat, your lordship," Mrs. Abbott bid. "Oh, no! This settee is much more comfortable. I mean to dispose of that one there and replace it."

Mildred gave him a curious look as she returned with the tea.

"Oh, surely we have better biscuits than these!" Mrs. Abbott exclaimed.

"Alas, we do not," Mildred replied.

Mrs. Abbott colored. "Well, we shall be sure to add biscuits to our list. Perhaps we have some fruits we can offer his lordship?"

"I require no refreshments. The tea is sufficient," he said.

Mr. Abbott appeared just as Mildred had finished pouring the tea. When she handed Alastair his cup, their fingers brushed. A blush seemed to rise in her cheeks and she quickly retreated.

"Your lordship," greeted Mr. Abbott, "you are most welcome in our home, always, but is there something I can assist you with?"

Alastair stared at Mildred as she busied herself adding sugar and milk to her tea. The sugar surprised him, for he had noticed at Edenmoor, she did not take sugar, possibly in protest of the slavery used to provide it

"Indeed, your presence honors us," added Mrs. Abbott. "Were you in the neighborhood then?"

Mildred glanced at her mother as if to say that no business would bring the Marquess to Cheapside.

"Forgive my unannounced appearance," Alastair said, "but I had thought to inquire if the dowry I am bequeathing your daughter will be needed this year?"

"Oh, we had hoped so!" Mrs. Abbott replied. "But Mr. Carleton may not return till spring of next year."

Alastair noticed Mildred was only half successful in suppressing a grimace. "Mr. Carleton?"

"He is a gentleman engaged in much trade in the West Indies, and alas, he is required there to oversee some troubles." She looked to her husband. "But we expect that a proposal will be coming upon his return."

Mildred did not seem to share the excitement of her mother.

"I shall have to look into this Mr. Carleton," he said. "As the provider of Miss Abbott's dowry, it is in my interest to see the funds bestowed upon a worthy man."

"Yes, of course, and we cannot thank you enough for your generosity. Indeed, it is beyond generous. I should say it were saintly—"

Mildred coughed, and even Mr. Abbott, aware that Alastair found verbosity tiresome, attempted to gesture for his wife to cease.

"I would hazard, however, that Miss Abbott has many suitors?" Alastair asked.

Mildred met his stare. "Is it Mr. Winston that concerns you?"

He appreciated her bluntness. "Hedoes, Miss Abbott. Mr. Winston has a suspect past, and I think it wise to stay your distance from him."

"I knew it!" Mrs. Abbott cried. "I knew he was not worthy of Millie."

"He is a friend of the Grenvilles, Mama, and I do not think they would associate themselves with someone of questionable character."

"He is staying with Mr. Harris, who is a friend of the Grenvilles. That is different."

Mildred turned to Alastair. "What do you have to support your judgment?"

"Sufficient details exist to warrant my disapproval. The death of a young woman may be placed on his conscience."

Mrs. Abbott gasped.

"I know of this already," Mildred declared.

Alastair stared at her in disbelief while Mrs. Abbott made another gasp.

"And you are not troubled by this?" he asked.

"He admitted full responsibility to me, and perhaps if you had granted him the opportunity to speak his side of the matter—"

"It would not alter my opinion of him."

"But are you certain you do not form your opinions too quickly?"

"Millie!" Mrs. Abbott cried. "I doubt his lordship would speak ill of anyone lest he had reason. I am certain you are a great judge of character, my lord."

"Miss Abbott, on the matter of Mr. Winston, I will not support any suit of his."

"What if he were to convince you that he could make a good husband?"

"How would he do so?"

She furrowed her brow. "He could have married any number of eligible women from families of means."

"Perhaps, but are you certain they would have him?"

"Millie, why are we discussing Mr. Winston?" Mrs. Abbott asked. "His lordship has made known his opinion."

"His opinion may be misplaced," Mildred replied. "Perhaps if he took the time to better acquaint himself with Mr. Winston—"

"You may save your breath, Miss Abbott. I have no desire to better acquaint myself with Mr. Winston."

"But then how will he prove himself to you?"

"That is not a concern that troubles me. But there is one way to prove his intentions. Let us remove the dowry and see if his interests remain true."

Mildred straightened in indignation. "I am certain it shall! Despite what you may think of him, avarice is not a prevailing trait."

Her ready defense of Winston vexed him, and he made no reply.

"There, that is the wisdom of Solomon," Mrs. Abbott praised.

"Mr. Carleton began to take an interest only after my dowry had been raised," Millie said, "yet you do not condemn him."

"I will look into the character of Mr. Carleton," Alastair voiced, "but Mr. Winston will not have a penny of your dowry."

"It will not matter to him!"

Alastair tightened his grip on his teacup. This was madness. Why was she so stalwart in her defense of the man, especially if she knew his past?

"You would marry without a dowry?"

"I would."

Mrs. Abbott looked horrified. "Millie! Stop this nonsense! Mr. Abbott, you have heard his lordship. You would not approve a proposal from Mr. Winston."

"No, of course not," Mr. Abbott answered. "I have the highest regard for Lord Alastair. And as he is the benefactor, his opinion prevails."

Alastair looked back to Mildred. He saw a stubborn set to her jaw, but she made no further objections. Having made himself clear, he indicated he would take his leave. Mrs. Abbott attempted to persuade him to stay, till Mr. Abbott told her that surely his lordship had more important matters than to while away the time with them, to which Mrs. Abbott then heartily agreed and said that they would not detain him further.

Mildred bid him farewell with a silent curtsy, but he noticed the frown upon her countenance had not left her. As the carriage took him back to Mayfair, Alastair considered if he should have divulged more details of Winston's past. He should not have had to. Millie's parents had given no objections. But Millie had remained steadfast in her own opinions of Winston. Perhaps the reason she was blind to the man's possible faults was because she had fallen in love with him. The thought made Alastair grind his teeth.

Her reactions concerned him greatly. More needed to be done to address the situation.

CHAPTER TWENTY-EIGHT

"THIS IS MOST UNFORTUNATE," MRS. Abbott declared. "What will her ladyship think?"

"Millie does look pale," Mr. Abbott said. "Come, we had best depart soon or we shall be late."

"Give my regards and, of course, my regrets to Lady Katherine," Mildred said weakly from her bed.

"How is it you should fall ill on Christmas!" Mrs. Abbott lamented for the fourth time, but, with many sighs, she followed her husband.

When Mildred heard the sound of their carriage pull away, she leaped out of her bed and dressed in better traveling clothes. She pulled out the valise she had packed earlier. It was a small one and could only fit a few of her garments, but a larger one would prove too cumbersome. She had a few hours to make her way to the designated posting inn outside London. From there, she and Mr. Winston would make their way to Gretna Green.

"Elope?" Mr. Winston had echoed in great surprise when she had intercepted him a few blocks from the Abbott home earlier that day. "Am I not to ask your father for your hand in marriage?" .

"It is the only way," she had explained. "Father will not give his consent. Not after Alastair threatened to retract the dowry."

"Retract the dowry? Are you certain?"

"He came to tea yesterday and spoke quite forcibly. He claims he heard complaints of your character in your time at Oxford, but when I pressed him for specifics, he provided none and admitted he has no direct knowledge of you."

"That is distressing to hear," Winston had said, appearing deep in thought. "I own I was hardly perfect in my youth, but what he had heard must have been quite serious for him to make such a declaration."

"Well, it matters not. I asserted that you were not the sort to marry for money. Alastair deserves a proper scolding, but it is useless, he pays little heed to anyone."

"There must be some way to convince him that I have only honorable intentions toward you."

"He believes that removing the dowry is the only way to prove you truly care for me."

Troubled, he furrowed his brow. "But eloping will not improve matters. We had better attempt to reason with your cousin."

"In truth, I have no desire to. I had asked him to retract the dowry long ago. I've no wish for his money. It only affords him the opportunity to interfere in my affairs. You say you have sufficient income for a modest living, and I have no wish for more. I am quite accustomed and content with a humble life, and making economies does not frighten me."

"Millie, eloping is no small matter and will greatly upset your family."

"The sort of man they wish me to marry would certainly make me unhappy. I could not do it. It is my hope that, in time, my mother and father will love me enough to forgive me."

George had continued to make other arguments against eloping, but she was determined and eventually wore him down. She appreciated that he was concerned for her welfare and her honor, but the sooner she set upon her new path in life, the better.

"We could be wed within the day at Hyde Park Corner..." she suggested.

"No, no, if we are to elope, we ought to—perhaps—well, let us make it a grand adventure and make for Gretna Green."

"Gretna Green? Is that necessary?"

"We should go where we cannot be found till after we are wed."

Mildred nodded. "Very well. I do not require much packing."

"And we should meet outside of London so that we are not seen by anyone known to us. There is an inn on the road to Scotland, the Boar's Head."

They agreed to meet on Christmas, when her family would be with Lady Katherine and not notice her absence for many hours. That night at dinner, Mildred could barely eat as she considered how much she would miss her mother and father, and what their reactions must be when they discovered what she had done. She trusted her father would not disown her, but it might be some time before she would be admitted into their house.

Lady Katherine, too, would be wounded that she had not been brought into Mildred's confidence, but Mildred feared her ladyship's discouragement. Though Lady Katherine might form a favorable opinion of Mr. Winston, and Mildred suspected she would, her ladyship would undoubtedly urge patience, perhaps even offering to speak to Alastair.

But Mildred wanted an end to the tormenting feelings that gripped her whenever she thought of her cousin. In truth, she had fallen a little in love with him at Château Follet. She had not wanted to acknowledge it, and their time at Edenmoor had only deepened her feelings for him.

Mildred slept fitfully that night. Christmas morning could

not arrive soon enough.

"IT IS CHRISTMAS DAY, MY lord," said Alastair's house-keeper.

"Food and money, then," Alastair replied to her inquiry as to what should be given to the wassail before dismissing her. He remained seated behind his writing table but retained a view of the gentleman who sat opposite on the sofa. "Do you love her?"

"I have a great fondness for Miss Abbott," Winston replied after a pause.

Alastair stared at the man as if he could see past the façade and into his heart.

"I care for her greatly and would endeavor to make her happy to the best of my effort," Winston added. "That would seem sufficient to qualify for love."

Alastair felt his body tighten. His next question was the more difficult one. "And does she love you?"

Winston was more quick to answer this one. "Yes, and I am grateful and honored to receive her affections."

If the quill he held had been made of sturdier material, it would've snapped beneath Alastair's grip.

"A man of your charms could have a woman of superior qualities."

"You flatter me, my lord, but I am more than content with Miss Abbott. She is an intelligent creature, and her company quite enjoyable."

"She is of middling beauty, her figure imperfect."

"I do not see that to be the case, my lord. She may not have the loveliest of countenances and her form is perhaps not so slender, but I would not say she is not comely."

"Her family is of inferior breeding."

"My family is not so superior that I would criticize her background. She is fortunate, however, to be connected to your family."

"The benefits are not as great as they may seem. I erred in my generosity with her, and thus have reconsidered the dowry I was to provide her."

"May I ask what has prompted this decision?"

"It has come to my attention that her dowry has attracted unsavory suitors. If the dowry is lacking, then we may be assured that the man who still wishes to marry her is sincere in his affections."

"What of her happiness?"

A muscle rippled along Alastair's jaw. Of all men, why had she chosen Winston?

"I am willing to care for her as well as any man can care for his wife. And if she would be happy with me, I fail to see the wrong in this."

"Then you would wed her without a dowry?"

Winston said nothing and would not meet his eye. "I do not think it wise for us to marry in that case."

"Without a dowry, she no longer holds your interest. I think I see the extent of your affections, sir."

Winston looked up at him. "You would punish a member of your own family in so harsh a manner?"

"She is a cousin by marriage only, and marrying you, sir, would be the greater punishment."

Winston drew in a sharp breath. "Does her happiness mean so little to you?"

"Are you so certain she will be happy with you?"

"She loves me."

"You are certain of this?"

"She does not care for your dowry. She will have me without it. Indeed, we plan to elope. Today, in fact."

Alastair leaped to his feet. "Elope? On Christmas? I find it hard to believe that Miss Abbott would disrespect her family in this manner."

"Perhaps you underestimate her affections for me."

Alastair wanted to wring the man's neck.

"It was her idea. I tried to dissuade her from it. I had thought it would be more reasonable to attempt to persuade you the virtues of our marriage, but she was adamant."

"And you mean to see this elopement through?"

Winston straightened. "I may yet convince her to abandon her impulsive suggestion."

Alastair narrowed his eyes. "You have no desire to marry Miss Abbott without her dowry."

Winston lifted his chin. "Perhaps I will elope with her."

"I think not, for if it is funds you seek, I will make it worth your while to stay your distance from her: an annuity of a hundred pounds a year. Marry her and you will have nothing."

"That is a paltry sum, especially for a man of your means."

"It is more than you're worth, but marry Millie, and you receive nothing. Or would you prefer that I bring all my resources to bear against you? If I choose to, I can see you turned out of every door in polite society."

Winston's bottom lip quivered. "I accept your proposal, Lord Alastair, and will let Miss Abbott's happiness fall upon *your* conscience."

Alastair drew the note he had prepared and thrust it into Winston's hands. "That is your first installment. You may communicate with my solicitor hereafter. Now get out before I throw you out."

Winston did not need to be told twice and strode out with as much dignity as a man of his character could bear.

Alastair fisted his hand, regretting he had not been given a provocation to box the man's ears in. He went to sit at his table but was too restless to remain seated.

Damnation.

Though he was glad to have rid Millie of Winston, he doubted she would be pleased at his intrusion. She did not understand that he acted for her benefit.

Her commitment to Winston still stunned him. Mildred was not the sort of silly young woman to fall in love with a handsome face and charming manners. Only one explanation remained for why she would disregard what he had done in his time at Oxford: she was deeply in love with the man.

His chest constricted at the thought, and he felt an ache surge in his groin. Winston was the last man he would see Millie with. Though he doubted this Mr. Carleton would be any worthier, if he had earned her contempt. He could think of no man he would be content to see her marry, but, for her sake, he would make an effort to see the better qualities in her other suitors. He did not wish to see her unhappy. If she knew the sincerity of his intentions, she might better be able to forgive him.

He rang for his hat and gloves. The Abbotts would be with Katherine for Christmas dinner.

CHAPTER TWENTY-NINE

KATHERINE HAD DECORATED HER HOME in holly, rosemary and ivy. As he took notice of the greenery, Alastair wondered why Katherine had chosen to celebrate Christmas with more fanfare this year rather than confine the holiday to the customary acts of charity.

"What a pleasant surprise," Katherine remarked. "I have hopes that perhaps you mean to amend your strained relations with your family."

"Such efforts are better aided by my absence rather than my presence," he replied.

He greeted the family members already present: Edward, his wife and sons; Harriet, her husband and newborn babe; his sisters and their husbands.

When he came to the Abbotts, he inquired, "Where is Miss Abbott?"

"Alas, she took ill after the Christmas service," answered Mrs. Abbott.

Guilt twisted in his bosom. Had she fallen ill from a broken heart after learning that she was not to wed Mr. Winston?

"She seemed weak during the service, "Mr. Abbott said to his wife. "I hope it is nothing serious."

Alastair frowned. "When did your service conclude?"

"I would say eleven o'clock."

"And she was already ill?"

"She was slow in her steps and put her hand often to her brow."

"She would have made every effort to come," said Mrs. Abbott, "if she were not feeling so poorly."

Alastair recalled that he had met with Mr. Winston about one o'clock. Her illness then was not due to the news Mr. Winston had to break to her.

This provided no solace to Alastair, for something seemed amiss. Millie and Winston had planned to elope today. Would Winston still intend to do so despite the offer he had accepted?

Alastair pulled his aunt aside. "Have you heard from Millie?"

"Not in some time, though I had invited her to tea several times."

"She has not written you? Or spoken of a man named George Winston?"

"I have heard nothing from her. In truth, I'm quite surprised that I have not, but I understand from her mother that she has been busy entertaining various suitors. Who is this gentleman you speak of?"

"A man not worthy of being called a gentleman." A sense of urgency haunted him. "They had planned to elope today."

Katherine blinked in surprise. "Elope? Millie? This is unlike her. And not to have said a word to me. I am astonished."

"Are you? But you were not astonished that she would go to the Château Debauchery with you?"

"That is different. An elopement will alter her life. How do you know of this Winston fellow and their elopement?"

"Because I had expressly forbid her continued acquaintance with him and threatened to revoke the dowry if they married."

"You said this to her?"

"And to her parents. Winston is a dangerous fellow."

Katherine furrowed her brow. "In what manner?"

"In the severest of manners."

"Millie is unaware of this?"

"She is not, but would have him nonetheless." His whole body tensed. "She must be quite in love with him."

His aunt stared at him keenly. "And that vexes you?"

"That she would disregard my advice and elope with a man who will most certainly cause her ruin or grief? That she would fail to appreciate my generosity in providing for her dowry by running off with Winston?"

"And is that all that troubles you?"

"What do you imply, madam?"

"You think I do not know what happened during Michaelmas?"

He started. He was in disbelief until she smiled.

"I had hoped to speak to Millie about what transpired. She had seemed dispirited after you left Edenmoor. I thought perhaps she had fallen in love with you."

"Millie? With me?"

"And you with her."

He straightened. "Madam, you are a romantic."

"Do you deny it?"

"Even if true, it is of no consequence. Millie is in love with Winston, and I fear they may carry out this elopement. "

"If he is as bad as you say, you must stop them."

He nodded. "But speak not of this to Mr. and Mrs. Abbott. I do not wish to alarm them unnecessarily. I will take my leave without bidding adieu to the others."

"Of course. Godspeed, Alastair."

He could not receive his garrick, hat and gloves fast enough. When his carriage pulled up before the Abbott residence, he was out the vehicle before it had come to a complete stop.

"Where is Miss Abbott?" he asked the maid who answered

the door.

"In her room resting," the surprised woman replied.

He whisked past the servant. "I will see her—in her room, if she is too ill to leave it."

"Shall I take your hat and gloves, sir?"

"No, but please inform her that her cousin is here."

The maid nodded and went upstairs. He paced the vestibule while he waited. If Millie was asleep, he would wait until she wakened.

But what he had feared was true.

"She is not in her room," the maid said when she had returned.

Alarm gripped him. "Where are the other servants? Have they seen her?"

"I am the only one. There is a laundry maid whocomes once a week, but as it is Christmas, she will come tomorrow."

Wanting to confirm for himself, he took the stairs three steps at a time and went into the room with the open door.

It was empty. She had left. With Winston.

Alastair was stunned. Had Winston played him for a fool and only pretended to accept the offer of the annuity? Had he underestimated what partiality the man may have had for Millie? Or perhaps Millie had convinced him that the better course still lay in elopement. Millie was surprisingly persuasive. He ought not have underestimated *her.*

"Have you searched the rest of the house?" he asked the maid as she came up behind him.

"I have not. Should I? I don't understand. Miss Abbott was too ill to leave her bed."

"Where does she keep her coat?"

"Her coat, sir?"

Alastair opened the doors of an armoire.

"Oh!" the maid gasped in surprise. "It is not there."

"Are all her bonnets and shoes accounted for?"

The maid examined the rest of the armoire's contents. "How strange! Perhaps the laundry maid had come early this week?"

Alastair needed no further evidence. Millie was gone.

As disbelief faded, a sense of loss took its place. If she succeeded in marrying Winston, she was gone for *him*.

It was what he wanted, Alastair reminded himself. He had doubled her dowry so that she could easily find a husband and he would be done with her, but she had been right. Her dowry had attracted too many suitors, including undesirable ones.

He could not let her marry Winston. If he should find her before they married, he vowed he would make finding the best man he could for Millie his utmost priority. Or he could—

An object upon the floor caught his eye. The maid had missed the note that had perhaps fallen off the bed. Bending down, he picked up the note and unfolded it.

My Dearest Parents,

Please know first and foremost that I hold you in much regard and love. My present actions may appear to contradict this assertion, and perhaps it is my selfishness, and not a lack of esteem or love for you, that wins the day. I wish I could be a better daughter. I wish I could envision myself married to Mr. Carleton or any of the other men you would deem in my interest to marry. Alas, I cannot. I expect my greatest chance for matrimonial happiness lies with Mr. Winston. He is a good man whose disposition matches my own. I hope you will one day come to forgive the actions I feel compelled to take. I do so with a heavy heart at the pain this must cause you.

*I will send word when Mr. Winston and I are married.
He assures me that his situation is more than capable of
sustaining a modest living. I have never wanted much
more. Thus, you need not worry of providing for me. I
hope that you will consider welcoming us into your house
as Mr. and Mrs. Winston.*

*With love,
Mildred*

Pocketing the note, he asked, "Mr. Harris. He is a friend of
the Grenvilles. Do you know where he might live?"

"I know not, but the Grenvilles live at Cavendish Square."

He cursed, for he would have preferred to go straight to
Mr. Harris'. After telling the maid that there was naught to
worry and that he knew where Millie was—it was only a
temporary fib, as he fully intended to find Millie—he hurried back to his carriage and made for Cavendish Square.

He found the Grenville residence, and, to his fortune and
immense relief, Mr. Harris and Mr. Winston. Upon setting
eyes on the latter, he found it hard not to stride over and
deck the man.

"Lord Alastair—" Mr. Grenville began.

"I will have a private word with Mr. Winston," he growled.

Mr. Grenville showed them into the library. As soon as
the doors were closed, Alastair shoved Winston to the wall,
closing his hand about the man's throat.

"Where is she?" he demanded.

Winston gripped his arm, attempting to keep it from
crushing his neck to the wall. "What do you mean, sir?"

"Millie. Where did she go after you spoke with her?"

"I didn't."

Alastair felt the veins at this temple throb. "What? You did
not speak with her?"

"I did not wish to make a scene."

"If you did not speak with her, then she still thought you were to elope?"

"I sent a note to her."

Millie must not have received it. "Where? When?"

"At the Boar's Head Inn off the main posting road to Gretna Green."

"Gretna Green! Why the devil would you travel that far? You are both of age. Why not marry at Hyde Park Corner or even Fleet?"

"It was her idea! Their sex thrives on romanticism!"

Alastair tightened his grip before throwing Winston to the ground in disgust. If he had the luxury of time, he would throttle the man. But he wanted to get to Millie.

"You will not speak of this to anyone, save that you and I had a disagreement to settle. If you wish to demand satisfaction, name your seconds," he said to Winston, who remained on hands and knees.

When Winston only stared at him as if he were mad, Alastair threw open the doors and stalked past the surprised host. When in his carriage, Alastair let out an oath that even startled his driver. He could not believe that Winston had not spoken or, at the least, written a letter to Millie at her home. Instead, he had allowed her to travel to a posting inn on her own.

The fucking bleeder.

The carriage could not arrive at the posting inn fast enough. As few people traveled on Christmas, the innkeeper was properly astonished to see Alastair.

"I seek a young woman," he informed the elderly keeper when he did not see Millie.

"I had a young woman here earlier. She was alone and sat for several hours, till a letter arrived by messenger for her."

"Do you have the letter?"

"It is with her. I saw her place it in her reticule."

"What happened then?"

"After readings its contents, she asked if there would be a coach today. I said not likely, as it was Christmas. My son was visiting and had himself a wagon. I offered that he could take her where she wished to go for the right price."

"And where did she wish to go?"

The man furrowed his brow. "Can't remember, as I never heard the name before."

Alastair drew in a breath to calm his patience. He was ready to wring the innkeeper if it would do any good.

"They took the road that leads to Surrey."

Surrey. Why would Millie head in that direction? Alastair understood that she no longer needed to head north to Gretna Green if the letter the innkeeper referenced was the one that Winston had written, but what lay to the southeast?

He stiffened as the answer came to him.

Château Follet.

CHAPTER THIRTY

---◈◈◈---

"YOU ARE NO IMPOSITION, *MA cherí*. Of course you must stay," Madame Follet said, greeting Mildred in the salon. As always, the hostess appeared radiant in her white draped muslin, a vibrantly hued Turkish shawl, and golden jewelry. She carried herself with the vivacity of a young woman of twenty, despite being twice that in years.

"I could think of nowhere else to go," Mildred said, abashed.

"I am flattered you would choose to spend Noel at Château Follet. I have a number of guests here, and they would more than welcome an addition."

"A place to spend the night is more than sufficient."

"Nonsense! You cannot come here and not take part in the revelry. I have even prepared a special midnight feast, a *Le Reveillon* if you will, but of a much more wicked nature."

Gratitude filled Mildred. Madame Follet had not even inquired into why Mildred should have traveled here on her own.

"I cannot thank you enough, Madame Follet."

"I will have a room prepared for you, and mind the kissing boughs."

"Kissing boughs?"

Madame Follet pointed at the ivy with white berries that hung above the threshold. "It is a quaint practice, from the peasantry I believe. If you wish for more than kisses, do not hesitate to inform me if you are desirous of a partner. I would be happy to provide you one."

Mildred blushed. She had not considered participating and doubted she could be in the proper mood. Once settled in her own room—the very same she had stayed in her first time at Château Follet—she drew out the letter from Mr. Winston.

Dear Miss Abbott,

I regret that you shall be reading this, but I could not forgive myself if our marriage earned you the disdain of your family and, in particular, your cousin, the Marquess of Alastair. I would Lord Alastair had not threatened to take away your dowry, but you are deserving of a man who can both make you happy and keep your dowry.

G.W.

She sighed at the brevity of the letter and how it had made no mention of his affections. Yet, the letter had not caught her completely by surprise. The look in his eyes when she had informed him that Alastair intended to revoke her dowry, and his hesitant reception of her idea to marry regardless of Alastair's approval, had been evidence of his true intentions, but she had failed to give them their due. Did he truly decide not to marry because he thought she would be better without him? Or had she misjudged his partiality for her?

Tearing the letter in twain, she cast it into the hearth.

Since Christmas service this morning, she had vacillated between heartache and anticipation. Perhaps she could have made it back to London before her parents had returned from Christmas dinner with Lady Katherine, but, at the time, she'd had no desire to return home in defeat. She realized now that she was given to impulsiveness, and perhaps, as with accepting Haversham's proposal, she had been rash. She had wanted to be the good daughter, but in the end, she had not the fortitude to see it through. Disgrace and shame certainly awaited her now.

And she had thought she could not commit a worse mistake than accepting Haversham's proposal.

Looking about, she found comfort in the familiarity of her surroundings. She had liked this room during her first visit, though she had not spent a great deal of time in it. The same pastoral paintings with but hints of lasciviousness graced its walls of rose-colored silk. She remembered how cheerfully the afternoon sun shone into the room, brightening the mahogany furnishings.

Bhadra, the comely Indian maid who had served her last time, appeared to assist her from her traveling clothes. When selecting a gown for the evening, Mildred hesitated at the ivory muslin she had thought she might wear when she wed Mr. Winston.

"You'll look lovely in this gown," Bhadra said, running her hand through the delicate top layer with burgundy embroidery at the hem. "You must wear it, miss."

"I suppose it is festive in appearance," Mildred contemplated.

To the gown, Bhadra added the pearls she had unpacked from the valise and did Mildred's hair in a loose coiffure. "Oh, miss, you do look lovely."

Mildred gave her reflection in the vanity looking glass a half smile. She could not look much better than she did.

"Will you be joining Madame downstairs? She said she would save you a seat beside hers."

Straightening, Mildred replied, "I think I shall."

She had no desire to nurse her sorrow alone in her chambers. As she was here at the Château Debauchery, why not benefit from some of its aspects?

Madame Follet was in a drawing room downstairs sitting on a sofa against the wall. With tapestries of gold, red, and turquoise, and pillows and rugs of equally vivid coloring, Mildred was reminded of a painting she had seen here at the château of a Turkish harem. In the center of the room, lounging upon the pillows, were two women. One wore only pantaloons of the sheerest fabric. The other had on a silk robe left untied, beneath which it was clear she had on nothing. She languidly caressed the full breasts of the first woman while a half dozen other occupants looked on.

"How wonderful that you could join us," Madame greeted Mildred. "And how ravishing you look!"

Mildred blushed a little. "It is Christmas."

"Sit with me a while. Would you like a ratafia or negus?"

Mildred opted for the latter, which had a strong taste of cinnamon and nutmeg. She sat and watched as the one woman began responding to the touch of the other.

"Have you had the pairing already?" Mildred asked of the ritual in which the guests who had come alone would seek their partners.

"Are you interested?"

"No, no," Mildred quickly replied.

"Because Francois, one of my footmen, would be more than happy to have the company of a lady tonight. Or Laroutte, my brother, said he would make himself available."

"Monsieur Laroutte?"

"You seem surprised."

"I thought him partial—well, I mean, I..."

"Thought him partial to men? He is. But on occasion he enjoys the fair sex. He remembers you."

Mildred flushed deeper. "You are a gracious hostess, but I am content to sit a while."

She watched as the second woman slid her hand down into the pantaloons of the first, seeking her mons. The first woman purred and reclined her back against the other. For several minutes, the second woman stroked the first. Mildred felt the area beneath her waist stir with sensation. She had never seen two women together before. As both women had nicely formed bodies, they appeared quite alluring.

The woman in the pantaloons turned her head, and their soft lips joined. Entranced with curiosity, Mildred forgot about her glass of wine. She wondered how two women would engage in congress. Would they employ a dildo or would they merely fondle one another with hands or mouth?

A young man with a woman on his arm approached. "Madame Follet, my wife and I wish to thank you for your hospitality. Christmas is not a holiday we observe with great festivity, but thanks to Château Follet, it is now our favorite holiday."

"I am pleased to hear it, Mr. Cornell. I wondered that you would attend this year, given how busy you have been with Parliament. May I congratulate you on your election."

He bowed.

"He is a newly elected MP from Middlesex," Madame explained after the couple had left, "and a proud—what do you term them—Foxite?"

"He does not worry that he will be discovered here?"

"He could not be more notorious than Fox himself was."

Mildred could not imagine any man with a career in the public realm would dare consider the debauchery of Château Follet. Nonetheless, she was intrigued, but as Mr. and Mrs. Cornell had left the room, Mildred returned to watching the two women. The first one was now taking her turn addressing the second, who lay upon her back, her robe pulled fully open to expose her creamy white breasts, which the former took to kissing and suckling. There was no denying the warmth that spread through Mildred. Though she doubted she could ever touch or wish to be touched herself by one of the same sex, there was both a beautiful and most wanton quality to a woman attending to another. And it aroused.

Madame Follet leaned toward her. "Are you quite certain you would not wish to pass the evening in the company of Francois or Monsieur Laroutte? Or perhaps you wish to try your hand with one of the fair sex?"

Mildred felt her pulse quicken. "I suppose…if Monsieur Laroutte is amenable…"

A S SHE WAITED FOR LAROUTTE, Mildred scanned the chambers, the one she and Alastair had played in. Located in the East Wing, reserved for the more *experienced* guests, the chambers could have passed for a medieval den of torture with its many cages, St. Andrew's cross, wooden pony, and table with paddles, floggers, and crops. After spending over half an hour observing the two women caress and fondle each other, leaving no inch untouched, lust warmed her own body. She was pleased with her decision to partake of the activities at the château. It would relieve her mind of Winston.

Hearing someone enter, she turned around—and nearly died. She would have preferred to die. For upon the threshold, closing the door behind him, stood not Laroutte but Alastair.

Her mind reeled. How could such a coincidence occur *twice?* She ought not be surprised that he would spend Christmas at Château Follet—it was a more probable destination than any other—but she still could not refrain from disbelief.

They regarded each other in silence for what felt like an eternity before she managed to swallow her trepidation and ask him, "What do you do here?"

He crossed his arms before his chest, his stare unrelenting. "I could ask the same of you?"

"Why— You are not at Christmas dinner with Lady Katherine?" she stalled. Her mind searched for a plausible answer, for she knew that he would not allow his question to go unanswered for long, but came up wanting.

"Why are *you* not?"

Of course he would ask the same of her. There was nothing left but to confess.

"You may be pleased to know that we need not concern ourselves any longer with Mr. Winston. You are correct. I think he wanted only my dowry."

Fearing that her voice would crack, she said no more.

His expression softened. "I would rather have been wrong."

She nodded, comforted a little by his remark, though she could not recall a more dreadful moment than this: facing her cousin after a failed elopement with a man he had advised against. If he gave her a set down for her silliness, or triumphed that he had been the wiser of the two, she would not fault him. She supposed she should have known that Alastair would be right, that he would have an intuition for these sorts of things, especially as he claimed to be a cad himself.

"I will not disturb your visit here," she assured him, hoping he would leave soon to tend to his own pursuits for the evening. When he did not move, she added, "As I am no longer a novice here, you need not concern yourself with me and may forget my presence entirely to enjoy the revelry."

"I did not come to Château Follet for the revelry."

She blinked several times. Had her family, upon discovering her note, sent him to fetch her?

"I came for *you*," he confirmed.

He sounded displeased. This would not do. She had no wish to return. Not now. Not until she had nursed her wounds by indulging in a night of debauchery.

"How did you know to find me here?"

"An educated supposition based on the information I obtained at the posting in."

"The posting in? How did you know...?"

" Winston told me of your ridiculous notion to go to Gretna Green."

"You—you spoke with him?"

"He came to see me in hopes of persuading me to reinstate your dowry."

Her heart sank further. Of course he did. She wondered if he had ever truly entertained the notion of marrying her sans a dowry or if it had all been a charade?

"I should have known my dowry was my finest quality," she murmured.

"Millie, you are worth far more than Winston."

The earnestness in his tone surprised her, and she was able to rally her spirits a little and proclaim, "I think after this, I am determined to remain a spinster."

She expected him to chuckle, and his crossness did appear to thaw a little. She wondered where Monsieur Laroutte had gone to?

"I suppose my family must be discouraged?" she asked after another spell of silence.

"Perhaps, as they will likely have discovered your absence by now."

"You did not...? You did not come at their bidding?"

"When I found you were not at Christmas dinner with my aunt, I suspected what was afoot, but I had no wish to alarm your parents. If I had arrived at the posting inn before you left, we could have returned back to London before your family was the wiser. But you chose to run off to Château Follet."

His tone made her flush.

"Why?" he demanded.

"Why not?" she returned.

"You promised not to return."

"It was a rather inane promise to make."

"Nevertheless, you made it."

She found it difficult to swallow. His pupils had constricted.

"And will now pay the consequences of breaking your promise," he finished.

CHAPTER THIRTY-ONE

A LASTAIR COULD SEE HER QUIVER. She looked exceptionally lovely tonight. The gown suited her. The décolletage did not dip particularly low; still, her breasts swelled nicely above it. He felt a wave of jealousy as he considered that it might have been Winston who had inspired her to appear this alluring.

He continued to seek in her countenance evidence of the extent of her grief, but she appeared, at present, to weather the devastating blow that Winston had dealt her with poise.

"She appeared a little downtrodden," Madame Follet had said when he had pressed the hostess for any insights Millie might have confided to her, "but far from despondent."

"Millie is too practical for melancholy," Alastair had replied, feeling some measure of assurance. Though he knew he had spared Millie a life of misery with Winston, he could not bear the sorrow he must have caused her.

"If she was taken with this Mr. Winston, I would have expected her to be much more disconsolate."

"Perhaps the shock of it has not dissipated."

"Or perhaps she does not love this man as much as you think."

He would have liked that to be the case, but why else would Millie have risked her reputation and disappointed her family?

As he stared at Millie, he was determined to drive out all thoughts of Winston.

"I will agree to no such thing," Millie declared.

"You broke a promise."

"You may exact another consequence, such as the revocation of my dowry."

"That has already been done," he said more harshly than he intended, but he was cross with her, despite his sadness for the wounds she had suffered both to her pride and her heart. Nonetheless, he would rather she had not sought to comfort her grief by coming to Follet to fuck another man. Bloody hell. Who would this woman not lift her skirts to?

And yet, he had to admire this similarity between them. He would have done no less had he been in her situation.

"You agreed not to return to Château Follet within the context of certain circumstances," he reminded her. "You will therefore uphold the arrangement under which you made the promise."

"I am expecting Monsieur Follet."

"He is engaged with another now."

Distress flared in her eyes. Trembling, she backed away from him as he advanced toward her. He had a dual purpose in what he did. He wanted her never to break a promise with him again, and her apprehension would take her mind off her broken heart. Removing his coat, he tossed it aside. He uncuffed his sleeves and rolled them up to his elbows.

Coming upon an armchair, she stepped behind it, though it would offer her little protection. When he reached for her, she slid from behind the chair toward the doors, but he caught her easily enough. Stumbling, she would have fallen to the ground if not for his grasp about her arm. She struggled to free herself and clawed him with her free arm. He dragged her over to the sideboard, where various restraints were kept. When she had regained her footing, she yanked harder. Grabbing the set of iron cuffs attached together by a short chain, he opened a shackle and cuffed it about her wrist, sending her into a panic. She kicked him while he secured a small padlock to the shackle.

"Alastair!" she cried.

"Behave yourself, and I may take mercy upon you."

She considered her options briefly, then opted to attempt escape.

He whipped her against the sideboard, pinning her in place with his body; pulled her other arm in front of her, and clamped the remaining shackle to her wrist. Adding a second padlock, he now had both wrists locked into the cuffs. She continued to struggle, her motions causing her arse to grind against his pelvis. Heat flared through him, pounding in his head.

"Alastair!" she protested again.

The sound of his name only fueled his ardor. Grabbing the chain between the shackles, he tugged her toward the rope-and-pulley system in the center of the room. She resisted by digging in her heels but only succeeded in stumbling and falling on her rump. He hauled her a few steps farther, and, hooking the tackle to the chain, was able to draw her to her feet by pulling on a rope.

"Stop!" she pleaded with equal parts indignation and desperation.

When he had her on her toes, he tied the end of the rope to a shackle mount on the ground.

"Alastair!

He seized her jaw. "Is this not what you sought in coming here?"

"Not with you," she managed to utter despite his grip upon her.

The blood drained from him. No. She had expected Laroutte, or would have had some other fucker. Devon if he were here.

But he would not let any other man have her. She belonged to him.

"You will have me all the same," he told her, no longer attempting to stay his anger.

"You're the most abominable man ever!" she cried when he had released her jaw. "If you have revoked my dowry, you have no standing to interfere in my affairs."

"*You* invited my interference first."

"Which has become the greatest regret of my life!"

"Has it?" He stood so that their bodies touched. He cupped a breast through her gown and stays. Leaning his mouth toward her ear, he whispered, "Your body might disagree."

Her breath grew uneven, and it seemed a moan would pass her lips. Instead, she kicked at him, but doing so placed the weight of her upon her arms. Grimacing when the bones in her hands pressed into the shackles, she quickly returned to the tips of her toes. He went back to the sideboard.

"I will tell Lady Katherine," she threatened.

"And you think I am daunted by this?"

"Madame Follet then. She may throw you out."

Tired of her protests, he selected a gag—one that had the appearance of a metal spider.

"She may, but I am willing to risk it."

When he returned to her, he saw the sparkle of fear in her eyes.

"Al—Alastair, this is madness!"

"I had not given you permission to use my name."

She paled.

"Do you require your safety word?" he asked.

"Wh…?"

When she made no further answer, he pulled down her jaw and slid the circular part of the gag into her mouth. He had given her the opportunity to use her safety word, and she had not chosen to use it.

After fixing the gag to her, he stepped back to admire how the mouthpiece stretched her lips, forcing the orifice open in a most wanton and inviting fashion.

"When I am through with you, you'll not think to break a promise to me ever again."

CHAPTER THIRTY-TWO

---◇◇◇◇◇---

WITH HER MOUTH FORCED OPEN, Mildred could not swallow—at least, not without difficulty. She should have spoken her safety word when she had the chance, but some devilry inside her would not permit it to be spoken. But this was *not* what she wanted, because she knew her body would betray her, would yield to his touch. And then she would be left yearning in body and heart.

But with her arms shackled and stretched above head, how was she to escape? What could she do? Though she agreed that she had to atone for breaking her promise, his imposition infuriated her. Did he not have the slightest pity for her situation? Or did it only matter to him that he was in the right? How had she even come to love this man?

Drawing upon her indignation helped to ease her fears. She had endured three nights with Alastair during Michaelmas. Thus, she could endure a single night at Château Follet.

She hoped.

But, due to the turmoil inside her, her body was on edge in a manner she had never before known. When he brushed the backs of his fingers along her arm, she shivered. His hand came to cup a breast, and she had to close her eyes to refrain from being overwhelmed by the sensation, from wishing he could palm her naked instead. Standing behind her, he covered her bosom with his hands and squeezed the flesh through her stays. She grunted and tried not to let his touch excite her. To teach her a lesson, he would no doubt draw out her arousal, leave her craving for fulfillment while denying her completion.

However, without arousal, the pain would be harder to bear.

His hands roamed her body, caressing her midsection, gripping her hips, pressing her belly, and eventually fondling her between the thighs. She had worn but two layers of petticoats beneath, and she could easily feel his fingers pressing into her through the fabric. She squirmed to loosen his access, but he stilled her with his other arm. One hand clamped down upon a breast; the other rubbed her folds.

No matter how tightly she kept her thighs together she could not stay his penetration. All the while, her calf muscles strained to keep her on her toes so that her weight would not pull upon her arms. Resistance, she suspected, was futile. The firmness of his grasp, his ability to alternate between light and heavy caresses, called to her desire in a manner she had only ever experienced with him.

He pulled up her skirts and grazed her bare thigh, causing the blood to throb in her extremities. She both relished and wanted to evade his touch. It was madness wanting such contradictions, as if her mind was at war with her body.

Gradually, he released her and went about removing the pins from her gown. She closed her eyes. *Dear God.* She was to be naked before him. The skirt of her gown pooled below her. He then proceeded to untie her petticoats. The bodice of her gown, however, was a challenge, for, with her arms tied above, it could not be slipped off of her. He stepped in front of her, and seeing the fire in his eyes made her melt. There was nothing more titillating than seeing the desire there.

His gaze dropped from hers to the bodice. Undaunted, he

gripped the décolletage in both hands and proceeded to rip the gown in half.

She squealed through her gag. Was he mad? She could not believe he would destroy her finest muslin. She tried to move away from him, but it was not easy to move on the tips of one's toes. The fabric ripped easily beneath his efforts and hung in tatters at her shoulders. Her stays, fortunately, laced in front, so he had but to undo the ribbon. He left her shift alone and went to pick up a flogger.

The falls landed on her derrière first, and she instantly recalled how she had ached at the paddling she received at Michaelmas. Her arse tingled at the memory, and she found herself yearning for a reprisal. After a few mild lashes at her buttocks, the flogger traveled around her thighs, then back to her arse, and up her back. Her body, warmed by his earlier caresses and the kisses of the flogger, was now ready for harsher blows. She yelped when he landed the flogger harder against her, but she found herself wanting the punishment. She wanted what he would do to her.

Tucking the flogger beneath his arm, he stood before her. The shift went the way of her gown. Tearing it open, he exposed her breasts, midsection and pelvis. Her breath quickened through her nose, for breathing through her mouth caused it to dry.

Taking the flogger, he fit the handle between her thighs. She shuddered as the ridges of the handle rubbed against her folds. For several minutes, he sawed the handle between her legs, using it to nudge her clitoris. His gaze did not leave her face, and she succumbed to the look in his countenance, the smolder in his eyes, the firm set of his jaw. The wetness of her desire began to coat the handle of the flogger.

"Remember that you are not to spend without permission," he said as he drew the flogger back.

She moaned. The flogger had distracted her from the stiffness in her calves. She had begun to alternate her weight between her toes and her arms. She caught the reflection of herself, her body stretched toward the rafters, her tattered clothing hanging from her. Only her garters, stockings, slippers, and pearls remained intact.

He grasped a breast, his fingers slowly digging into the ample flesh. Lowering his head, he captured the nipple in his mouth, sending currents to shoot from that bud to the heat collecting between her thighs. Her cunnie ached as he licked and sucked. He performed the same attention upon the other nipple. Soon, she was fit to burst. She wanted the flogger back between her legs—no, she wanted *him* between her legs.

Releasing the nipple, he went to a set of drawers and pulled out a chain with clamps on either end. Returning, he fixed these to her nipples. She would have ground her teeth at the pinching pain upon her little buds. He tugged on the chain lightly before returning to the chest drawers. He came back with a little weight attached to a hook. He set the weight upon the chain. She screamed as the weight pulled her nipples down.

"Do you require your safety word?"

She could not utter it even if she had not the gag. She breathed through the sharp pressure on her nipples till the initial flare of pain receded to a tolerable but persistent ache.

He repeated his query. She was tempted to nod, but she feared more what happened if she called an end to their engagement. She shook her head. She believed she could survive this.

Until he added the second weight.

She sobbed—no, she could not properly sob with the damned gag—for it felt as if her nipples might be torn off. How was it the clamps did not slip off? Her body bowed and arched in search of release, but the effect of the weights could not be avoided. It was best she not move at all, for the swaying of the weights pulled at her nipples.

Tears pressed against her eyes. Perhaps she was wrong. Perhaps this time would prove too much for her.

CHAPTER THIRTY-THREE

KEEPING A CLOSE STUDY OF her to see if she might require her safety word if she could speak it, Alastair saw the dewiness of her eyes, the whiteness of her knuckles as she gripped the chain between the shackles. He removed the gag and waited for her to utter the safety word. She did not.

Cupping the side of her face with one hand, he brushed away a tear that had escaped her eye. She impressed him, and despite her errors, he doubted he could find a more enjoyable submissive.

Reaching between her thighs, he stroked her. Her arousal hardened his already stiff cock. He wished he knew that he was the sole cause of her desire, that she would not be so aroused by anyone else. Her breath, erratic from the pain, grew more haggard still. He fondled her clitoris till she squirmed, though she tried to remain motionless so as not to disturb the weights. He moved his hand, coated with her nectar, to her mouth. She licked and sucked his fingers clean.

His cock throbbed. He wanted her more than he had ever wanted a woman before. But he wanted her to feel the same intensity. How could she consider marrying a man like Winston? Could Winston take her body to such heights, catapult her, through pain, to an even greater euphoria?

Withdrawing his hand, he asked, "Are you ready to behave?"

"Yes, my lord," she said weakly.

She gasped when he removed the clamps and weights from her nipples. He pocketed the implements in his waistcoat and poured her a glass of water, which he placed at her lips. She drank readily.

"Thank you, my lord."

Looking into her eyes, he was lost momentarily in their brightness, and this time he felt his bosom swell.

Recalling himself, he set the glass down. She looked ravishing in her current position, and he was tempted to wrap her legs about him and fuck her as she hung in midair. But he wanted to hear her beg for his cock. Hearing her need, her desire for him, excited him to the depths of his loins.

Lifting her, he unhooked her and set her on her feet. Her legs trembled, and before she crumbled to the ground, he swept her into his arms and carried her to the low four-post bed where they had made love before. After laying her down, he opened the locks to her shackles and removed them. When she was done rubbing her wrists, he pulled her arms through her torn garments. He had not intended to rip her clothing, though his ardor had appreciated the alternate outlet. He silently promised her that he would purchase an even finer gown, shift and stays. Indeed, he would gift her anything she desired.

To his satisfaction, he found her staring at his crotch and the bulge there. He remembered all too vividly how well she had swallowed cock at Edenmoor. But he was not yet done with her punishment.

"Fondle yourself," he instructed, then went to return the shackles.

He brought back four cords of rope and watched her. She toyed with her clitoris with one hand and rolled her breast with the other. She gasped when her thumb accidentally slid over her nipples. He smiled to himself. They were still sore.

Taking a leg, he untied her garter and slid off her slipper and stocking. He wrapped the rope about her lower thigh, then tied the rope to the nearest bedpost at the headboard. When he had affixed the other leg in similar manner to the other bedpost, she lay with her legs spread and her quim fully exposed. By tethering her legs to the bedposts behind her, he not only pulled her legs apart, he had them pulled back toward her head, causing her rump to round off the bed and give him a view of her anus.

With the two remaining cords of rope, he tied her ankles to the tops of the bedposts. Her fondling had slowed as she looked at her bindings, no doubt wondering why she was being trussed to the bed in such a manner.

He climbed onto the bed and knelt before her. Instead of searching for another cord of rope, he undid his neckcloth. Taking both her wrists, he bound them to the rococo head-board. His body hovered over her, and her nipples gently nudged at his waistcoat whenever she drew in a breath. He looked down at her.

"You look lovely in pearls," he said of the strands gracing her neck.

She returned a wry smile. "Thank you, my lord."

He palmed a breast before lightly tugging its nipple. She made a slight grimace.

"How did your nipple enjoy the weights?" he asked.

"Not at all, my lord."

He pushed himself up and off the bed and went to the table of floggers and crops. He selected a light bamboo switch.

"The body has numerous sensitive parts," he told her as he went to stand beside the bed. "The nipples, as you know, are one. The feet are another."

She raised a curious brow, then giggled as he ran a knuckle along the arch of her foot. But he did not intend to tickle her. He tapped the bottom of the foot with the switch before landing a sharp smack.

She cried out and flinched at the impact.

He struck her again. She exclaimed in surprise.

Unlike other parts of the body, the feet did not acclimate to the repetition of impact. Great force was not required to produce the desired effect, though one had to take care to avoid the more delicate parts of the foot.

She shrieked an oath when the switch stung the vault of a foot. The bed creaked as she strained against her bonds. After several minutes, he paused to take a look at her cunnie. Her wetness had dripped down her arse to the bed. Putting down the switch, he settled himself on the bed to apply his mouth to her. Her eyes rolled to the back of her head as he flicked his tongue at her clitoris. The scent of her arousal filled his nostrils. He would have to take her soon, for his cock was ready to burst with need.

"Sir—my lord," she gasped when he intensified his feasting, "you shall make me spend. Please. Oh God."

He could sense her resisting the tide of pleasure his mouth and tongue were coaxing upon her.

"*Please,* my lord," she whimpered.

He ceased his application and, taking the switch, got off the bed and attended to her other foot. As she was further aroused, she was better able to take more punishment this time. Nonetheless, after a spell, she began to plead.

"Enough, my lord. Please."

He struck her again.

"My lord! Enough!"

He wanted to remind her of her safety word, but it would be better if she recalled it on her own. She needed to practice the rules of engagement if she expected to do well at Château Follet, if she should play with another man.

No. She had promised not to return to Château Follet. As for the prospect of another man…he thought of the Viscount

Devon. What if the two should cross paths?

Alastair tightened his hold on the switch. He did not want to think of Millie with another man—any man, let alone the Devon bastard.

"Ahhh!" she cried out when the switch stung her once more.

Millie belonged to *him*. She was his. To torment, to pleasure, to torment with pleasure.

"Pearls!" she yelled after he landed another whack.

And the only way he could assure that she would be his and his alone was to marry her.

CHAPTER THIRTY-FOUR

⬦⬦⬦

MILDRED SILENTLY CURSED HIM. SHE had not wanted to employ her safety word but had not expected such light strikes upon the bottoms of her feet could hurt with such excruciation. The pain, however, did not diminish the desire still burning in her body.

Conscious of how wantonly she was splayed upon the bed, she stared up at the ceiling instead of meeting his eye. What was she to do now? What would *he* do?

She gasped when she felt his touch at her mons. Looking down, she saw that it was his cock. Anticipation surged within her. He had unbuttoned his fall and now stroked the head of his member against her. Her moan wavered as delicious sensations rippled between her legs. He teased her with light brushes of his length along her, touching his tip to her clitoris, pushing the crown of his cock at her folds but not enough to enter.

"Oh, God, Alastair," she whispered when she thought she could endure no more. "Please fuck me."

"Look at me, Millie."

She gazed at him. He had a hard set to his jaw, and she did not know if it was from displeasure with her or merely the tension of lust.

"You have my permission to spend," he told her, "but if you ever break a promise to me again, no word of safety will save you then."

Thrilled that she would get to spend, she nodded with enthusiasm. "I promise to never break a promise to you again."

His shaft was at her slit, and she tried to wriggle herself onto him.

"And I expect you'll never return here without my assent."

"Yes, yes," she replied, straining for penetration. She would go mad if she had to endure the vacancy in her cunnie much longer. "I will uphold my promise this time. Truly."

In dismay, she watched him pull away.

"Alas— My lord? Did I displease you? Do you doubt me? How may I convince you of my earnestness?"

He stood and pulled the chain and nipple clamps from his waistcoat pocket.

She paled. Her nipples were still sore, and she wondered if they would forever be erect after what they had suffered.

He dropped the clamps and chain beside her on the bed, then unbuttoned his waistcoat. Far too slowly for her, he shed his garments one by one. Her cunnie clenched with each removal of clothing. When he stood in naked glory at last, a most sightly form with his muscled legs and ridged abdomen, she would have thrown herself upon him if she were not still trussed to the bedposts.

He climbed onto the bed and knelt near enough that his thighs almost brushed her buttocks. He aimed his cock at her.

"Thank you, my lord, thank you. I shall not fail you again. I promise—and it is a promise I shall keep this time. Only, pray, do not keep me waiting any longer for your cock."

Glancing at the clamps and chain, he appeared to have an inspiration. He clipped one end to her tongue and the other to her folds just above her clitoris. The pinching of the clamp at her folds called her attention to her nether regions, to the hunger down there, the craving for his touch.

Then, finally, he sank his cock into her.

At that moment, there was nothing more exquisite than being impaled upon his member. Her cunnie clutched at his shaft, eliciting a groan from him. He pressed himself farther into her. The angle of her hips allowed him to penetrate deeply, and he buried himself to the hilt, till she could feel the hairs of his pelvis against her flesh. He untied the ropes from her ankles, allowing her to drop her lower legs. As he began a gradual thrust, he tugged lightly upon the chain with one finger.

"How hard do you wish to be fucked?" he inquired.

"Hahd," she responded.

"Extremely hard?"

"Yehh."

Releasing the chain, he circled her clitoris with his thumb till she was lost in a sea of warmth and pleasure. Then he shoved his hips at her. Her head bumped into the headboard, and he adjusted the pillows behind her before settling back onto his haunches.

"Hard," he said, and slammed his cock into her several times. With his thumb, he strummed her clitoris as he bucked his hips. It was more than she could bear. All sensation, from the nipping of her tongue to the pull of the ropes upon her legs to the soreness in her nipples, hurled her toward that carnal purpose. Her orgasm erupted with the violence of cannon fire. A blinding white glory flashed through her, followed by much quaking and shaking, the intensity of which left her in a state of quasi-delirium.

Bracing himself over her, he pounded himself fast and furious into her to achieve his own end. The bed rocked beneath the force of his motions and thumped against the wall. His brow furrowed, and soon he had reached his apex. She would have cautioned him to pull out before he spilled his seed, but she would not be understood with the clamp upon her tongue, and, in truth, a part of her wanted to take him in this manner, to have his essence inside her.

She could feel the heat of his mettle, mixing with her own fluids. He unclasped the clamps before allowing his weight to collapse atop her.

"My God, Millie," he breathed before a final shudder went through his limbs.

His satisfaction gratified her, and she would have embraced him with her arms and legs if she could. She wished she could remain joined to him forever, and for the time being, she would refrain from considering the grim truth that awaited her and relish the weight of his body against her and pretend that he was hers.

CHAPTER THIRTY-FIVE

———◇◈◈◈◇———

HE WOULD HAVE PULLED OUT of her, but the temptation to mark her for his own, to leave a part of him in the deepest part of her, prevailed. He had already decided upon marrying her; thus, if there should be consequences to their congress, she would be safe.

Safe. He liked the certainty that marriage to Millie afforded. Liked that he would have many more opportunities to fuck her as he just had. It was the most brilliant paroxysm he had ever had. The sight of her bound to the bed, her intimacy exposed to him, the pearls about her neck and the chain of the clamps bouncing off her body, had aroused him to new heights. He hoped she had spent with equal glory, and he vowed to bring her to rapture as often as she wished. And more.

He untied the neckcloth from her wrists and the ropes from her legs. Settling back into bed, he wrapped her in his arms as they lay upon their sides. He could see that she was weary. She pushed aside the pieces of her torn garments

"I will replace the gown," he assured her.

She nestled into his embrace. "Thank you, but it matters not."

"You will have a finer gown—and shifts and stays—whatever you wish to spend your pin money upon."

"Pin money?"

He breathed in the scent of her hair. "Though I suspect you are as likely to donate your pin money to Luddites and the like."

She sat up, leaving his arms, to his regret. "Pray, it is not necessary to substitute my dowry with pin money. I am quite pleased you have revoked my dowry. I assure you that, despite what my parents may say, I am better off without one."

He pulled her back down. "A dowry is unnecessary, but as the Marchioness of Alastair, you will want pin money."

She sat back up. "The what?"

"The Marchioness of Alastair."

She looked horrified. "My lord? I mean, Alastair—my lord—surely you jest."

"Have you ever known me to jest?"

Her horror grew, and she scrambled from the bed. "Why would I marry you? I mean, why would you marry *me*?"

He could not help feeling a little insulted by the intensity of her reaction. He allowed she was in love with Winston, but the Marquess of Alastair was hardly rubbish.

"You have no need to salvage my honor, Alastair."

"Then who will? Your journey to Château Follet has made it impossible to return home at a reasonable time. You will have to pass the night here. Have you considered what explanation you can offer your family?"

"I have not, but that is not your concern."

He could not believe what he was hearing. She would not take his dowry. Now she would not take his hand in marriage. It could not be because she found him repulsive—her body had given him plenty of evidence to the contrary.

"Millie, I may be far from a saint," he said, "but I am more worthy of you than Winston. He is not even deserving of the hundred pounds I gave him."

"What hundred pounds?"

"I offered him an annuity to stay his distance from you."

Her mouth fell open. "You *bribed* him?"

"I should have simply threatened him, but I knew money would move him."

"You're the reason he didn't come!"

"Do not delude yourself. He never had any intention of marrying you without a dowry."

She gasped, made a face, then began angrily collecting her garments.

"Millie, he accepted the annuity without hesitating a second. Why are you not vexed with him?"

He grasped her by the arm as she turned toward her petticoats on the floor.

"You flatter me once again, Alastair. I am pleased to know I could be forsaken for as little as a hundred pounds a year."

"I would have offered more if I thought the bloody bastard deserved it. Devil take it, I would have offered a thousand pounds a year, but I think it quite telling that he accepted my offer as it was."

Her shoulders sagged, but he still heard vexation in her voice. "You're right, Alastair. I hope it pleases you to know that you are right."

She wrested her arm from him and, taking up her petticoats, she tied them about her.

"I care nothing of that," he protested. "I wanted to see you safe from him. Though you are of a stronger constitution, I would not want what happened to Miss Jones to befall you."

"Who is Miss Jones?"

He started. "I thought you knew? She is the young woman he cast aside after getting her with child. She took her life afterwards."

Millie paused. "That was not how he had told it."

"That surprises me little, but he lost a good friend, Mr. Stanton, over the affair."

"I suppose I owe you an apology, then, and my gratitude for rescuing me."

She looked at her garments and realized they were too torn to wear. He gave her his shirt and began to dress as well.

"I do not require your apology or you gratitude," he told her, relieved that she sounded less angry. "However, I would that my generosity wasnot wasted upon you."

"I must seem an ungrateful wretch, and perhaps I am. You have been good to me, Alastair, even though I have not always deserved it."

He liked the look of his shirt over her. Her coiffure had come undone, but the blush in her cheeks remained. "You deserve far more than you allow for yourself, Millie."

A grateful smile tugged at the corners of her lips.

"And while you deserve better than a rogue such as myself," he continued as he slipped into his braces and reached for his waistcoat, "I hope you will find some comfort in being married to me. I daresay your parents and Katherine would be happy."

Her eyes widened, and the dread returned. She shook her head. "Alastair, you are far kinder and more munificent than anyone could have imagined, but your offer is unnecessary."

To his surprise, she turned on her heel and, carrying her garments in her arms, made for the doors.

"That may be, but—" He took several long and quick strides to catch her. "Millie!"

"You need not concern yourself with my wellbeing. I am certain I can find a situation to support me till my family has forgiven me."

She opened the doors and hurried down the corridor. In her haste, as she turned the corner, she bumped into a couple. Her articles of clothing fell to the floor.

"Your pardon!" the various parties cried.

Alastair bent down to assist Millie

"Lord Alastair, is it not?" the man asked. When Alastair made no reply, the man offered his hand. "Mr. Cornell, at your service. I represent Middlesex, and must say I was most pleased to hear that you had rejected the Farnsworth proposal regarding stocking frames. I think he may present a bill next year, but at least we were spared its consideration this year."

Her garments returned to her arms, Millie stood and stared at him.

"I look forward to serving in Parliament with you, your lordship," Cornell added before he and his companion continued on their way.

Alastair turned to Millie. Her eyes swam with emotion. "You did not support Farnsworth?"

"We had an agreement, you and I, did we not?"

"Yes, but I had bid you only to consider the subject more than you had."

"And I did. I went to Nottinghamshire and observed the conditions of croppers and weavers. Their numbers in the poor houses have grown. You inspired me to consider their cause with more compassion. The Farnsworth proposal provides no solution for their suffering. I still consider machine-breaking a wrong, but I could not send a man to his death for it."

Her countenance brightened with what he thought might be affection. Encouraged, he took her hand. "Millie, you could make me a better man."

"You are far better than you credit yourself."

"If you believe that, then there is hope in our marriage. If you think I will always assume the role of dominant as your husband and lord over you, I assure you that will not be the case." Even if he did, he doubted she would submit to it. She tried to pull away, but he kept his hold of her. "You have my permission to give me a proper set-down when I am found to be overbearing."

"Alastair, stop such talk. I don't understand—"

"You may love Winston today, but I will earn your affections."

"Alastair, you…Winston is…"

His face darkened. "You do not still harbor hopes that he will have you?"

"Not at all. I don't love him. I never truly loved him because I loved…" Distraught, she continued to yank her hand from him. "*We* can't marry!"

"Why not?"

"Because you're the Marques of Alastair."

"I do not fear the consequences."

"But—"

He pulled her into his arms. "If you do not love Winston, why will you not have me?"

Caught in his gaze, she seemed not to be able to speak. When she did, her voice was small and trembled. "Because I love you."

Relief flooded him. He wanted to shake her a little for the unnecessary distress she had incited. "And I thought you had a proper reason for refusing me."

"It *is* a proper reason! I will not allow you to make such a sacrifice on my behalf."

"It is no sacrifice."

"How is it not a sacrifice?" she persisted in arguing.

"Because I love *you*."

She started, then returned a doubtful look.

"And I mean it," he said, cupping her chin. Then, daring her to refute him, added, "As sincerely as you meant it when you claimed never to break a promise to me again."

Her bottom lip quivered. "Alastair…"

"Say that you will have me, Millie, and then we may enjoy what remains of Christmas day."

She followed his gaze up toward the ceiling, where a kissing bough hung.

Before she could say another word, he claimed her mouth, impressing his love through his kiss. Her lips parted willingly for him, and in that moment, he sensed the last of her resistance had given way, just as her body had submitted to him earlier. He kissed her with tenderness, with vigor and passion.

He never would have thought, when Katherine first orchestrated their encounter at Château Follet, that their path together would have ended in marriage. Perhaps Katherine had suspected its possibility, and though he did not appreciate her meddling, he would forgive her this one time. For he had in his arms a woman worthy of worship and whose body he would take great pleasure in exalting in all manner of wicked wantonness.

When he parted to give her a chance to collect her breath, he felt a familiar tug at his groin. He saw the same lust in her eyes, as well as affection.

"Merry Christmas, Alastair."

He smiled and crushed her to him in another forceful kiss before bidding her a Merry Christmas, too.

THE END

OTHER WORKS BY EM BROWN

ABOUT THE AUTHOR

E M BROWN IS AN AWARD-WINNING multi-published author of contemporary and historical erotic romance. She found the kinky side to her writing after reading stories at Literotica.com. She likes to find inspiration from anywhere and everywhere, be it classical movies, porn, embarrassing high school photos, her favorite Sara Lee desserts, and the time she accidently flashed an audience with her knickers.

For more wicked wantonness, visit
www.EroticHistoricals.com.

Printed in Great Britain
by Amazon

60967189R00141